M000031607

Conyee,

It was great meeting at the Cornell Alumni get together. Keep being creative!

Matthew [illegible]

DO NOT FEED THE CLOWN

BY

MATT NAGIN

TENTH STREET PRESS

THIS EDITION

Published by Tenth Street Press 2019

Cover design by Dominique Bloink

ISBN 10: 0-6484802-7-5
ISBN 13: 978-0-6484802-7-3

Also available in digital formats

ISBN 10: 0-6484802-6-7
ISBN 13: 978-0-6484802-6-6

TENTH STREET PRESS
MELBOURNE SEATTLE LONDON
www.tenthstreetpress.com
Email: contact@tenthstreetpress.com

“Rejection Letters For Famous Authors” originally appeared in *The Higgs-Weldon.*

“Confessions of A Potted Plant” originally appeared in *Points In Case.*

“A Misanthropic Guide to the Holidays” originally appeared in *The Satirist.*

“Insensitivity Training at Dunkin' Donuts” originally appeared in *Robot Butt.*

“Children Beg To Return To Cages” originally appeared in *The Daily Squib.*

“Suicide Is In Again” originally appeared in *The People’s Cube.*

“Four Hot Stock Picks From Satanwater Destructive Capital” originally appeared in *Points In Case.*

“In Defense of Sorority Slang” originally appeared in *Points In Case.*

“Love Now Traded on NYSE” originally appeared in *Humor Times.*

“Brutally Honest Marketing Copy” originally appeared in *Points In Case.*

DEDICATION

This book is dedicated to my grandma, Sylvia Nagin, an artist, a generous soul, and an inspiration to me. She will be missed but not forgotten.

WHAT PEOPLE ARE SAYING ABOUT MATT NAGIN

PRAISE FOR MATT NAGIN

"Brilliantly irreverent…"
—Lee Levitt, *The Jewish Chronicle*

"Ridiculously funny…a stellar success."
—Alexis Yoo, *Stagebuddy*

"Weirdly wonderful…outrageous."
—Richard Propes, *The Independent Critic*

"Delightful to watch…[Matt] really does steal the show."
—Zachary Flint, *The Great Movie Debate*

"Clever…innovative....[Matt] is playing with the form and getting great results."
—Rick Overton, *Emmy Winning Writer, Actor, and Comedian*

PRAISE FOR FROM THE FRIDGE TO THE CRACKERJACK BOX

"Nagin's short essays mix Frank Zappa, Lewis J. Carroll, and Monty Python together with post Beatnik wacky introspection… An automatic attitude adjuster for those who wish to use comedy to feel good and relieved of woes."
—Ferris Butler, *Former Writer on Saturday Night Live*

"Matt Nagin clearly has a unique, clever way

with words and storytelling. His collection of humorous works is a definite must have for everyone who has a sense of humor. There hasn't been anyone around this funny in a very long time!"

—Donna Siggers, *Author of "Broken"*

PRAISE FOR
BUTTERFLIES LOST WITHIN THE CROOKED MOONLIGHT

"Kerouac and Ginsberg also understood poetry as effusion, and Nagin seems to have learned much from these countercultural icons. Powerful verse from a writer of real talent."

—Kirkus Reviews

"More personal than W.H. Auden (The Shield Of Achilles), more gut-wrenching than Robert Frost (The Lovely Shall Be Choosers). Dystopian power in forty-five poems."

—Jim Bennett, *Jim Bennett Reviews (5 Stars)*

"It's a distinctive style Matt Nagin has and his book deserves…applause. This is a must read."

—Katie Lewington, *Flying Through The Pages Book Review (4.5 Stars)*

"Nagin delivers in stark and jarring completeness."

—Erin Nichole Cochran, *Readers' Favorite (5 stars)*

PRAISE FOR FEAST OF SAPPHIRES

"Nagin *feels* his work, writing it with gritted teeth, through a pen as sharp as a razor, and his cynicism is smart and infectious. Poetry of the highest quality."
—Matt McAvoy, *Matt McAvoy's Reviews*

"If you are a lover of poetry, you'll really enjoy what's inside this book."
—Lisa Binion, *Lisa's Writopia*

"Nagin's work easily gets four stars. Highly recommended."
—Jim Bennett, *Jim Bennett Reviews* (4 Stars)

"This collection is full of riches...one of the best I've read in a while."
—P. D. Dawson, *P. D. Dawson Reviews* (5 stars)

NOTEWORTHY READER REVIEWS

"Excellent stuff! Nagin's book is the real deal. If Harlan Ellison were a poet, this is the book he would write."
—Larry Ryals

"Intense, enthralling, and wonderfully amusing."
—Barry Dayton

"Verses of boyish splendor."
—Elisa Hui

"Edgar Allan Poe with Balls!"
—Todd Montesi

"I keep rereading these texts and would like to share how inspirational they are."

—Julio Arraes

MATT HAS BEEN BANNED ON FUNNY OR DIE! TO FIND OUT WHY HIS ACCOUNT WAS TAKEN DOWN KEEP READING!!!!!

THE CONTENTS

Go Fund My Extraterrestrial Law Suit

$8.50 of $12,000,000,000,000
Raised by 2 people in 86 days

HELP SUPPORT MATT NAGIN, A MAN ABDUCTED BY ANGRY EXTRATERRESTRIALS

Note: Help us reach our funding goals! We're now accepting the following payment methods: Cash, Credit, Check, Money Order, Bank Wire, Promissory Note, Collectibles [no corny action figures please], Goat Herds, Legal and Illegal Tender, Human Kidneys [on ice only], Real and Fake Gold, Blood Oath [or a pledge to Satan], Bitcoin, Gift Certificates, and an All-Inclusive Vacation To Bora Bora.

<u>Story</u>

On July 4th 2015, while friends watched fireworks and barbecued in the park, I was abducted by The Klongors—vile, belligerent twelve-foot aliens. These heartless, malformed bastards repeatedly sexually assaulted me.

It was nightmarish. They fastened my arms to a trapezoidal gurney and made weird noises in my ear most closely resembling a pigeon having a heart attack. Telepathically, they filled my dreams with slime (my nights were a cross between *You Can't Do That On Television* and *Saw III)*. Worst of all they performed the dreaded anal probe (which is best described as a colonoscopy with a scope larger than a heating pipe).

After seemingly endless torture, I was dumped in a cornfield outside Parsippany, New Jersey. It was only after years of psychotherapy and several stints at Meadowview Psychiatric Hospital that I managed to return to my head waiter position at Fuddruckers (where I no longer serve Original Fudds Burgers with quite the same joie de vivre). As if all this was not enough, I seemed to enjoy parts of the anal probe—if I'm to be completely honest—and now have an intense fear that I'm gay (my church pastor suggests castration at St. John's Episcopal Hospital).

The physiological impairments were equally debilitating. It took years of physical therapy before I could stand up without clutching my side and groaning. Today, by the grace of God, I can walk again—albeit with a limp (when doing so I most closely resemble a clueless tourist who got gang raped by gay droogs in outfits straight out of *A Clockwork Orange*). What is more, the Klongors used highly unsanitary tools, and, as a result, I have ongoing gastrointestinal issues (I crap my pants more often than a toddler overdosing on Miralax).

My intention is to sue the Klongors, the MS-13 gang of The Whirlpool Galaxy. But my lawyer tells me sexual assault regulations work very differently 23 million light years from Earth. The Klongors have no concept akin to #metoo, which they consider even dumber than our infomercials on QVC. Victims of sexual assault are perennially ignored on Klongonia, particularly when unsubstantiated, hyperbolic claims are shared on Wongaziland, their version of Twitter. What is more, on Klongonia, an anal probe is considered an act of generosity for which you should arrive bearing gifts.

At the behest of my lawyer, I subpoenaed the Klongors to appear in NY State Supreme Court—an ineffective proposition to say the least. Not only did they ignore all court injunctions, my friend at S.E.T.I. couldn't solicit so much as a lowly radar signal. Hence, I've begun pursuing my only other option—raising funds to travel to Klongonia, where matters are settled via Slime Teleportation Contest (the more slime you teleport the bigger the financial retribution).

My idea is to tweak a Space X rocket to travel in hyperdrive on unleaded gas (since the RP-1 and LOX [liquid oxygen] Elon Musk normally employ are way out of my budget). Ancillary expenses include spacesuits, astronaut ice-cream, a Blu-Ray DVD player (there is no Netflix once you pass Pluto), and intergalactic parking tickets.

Please understand my plans are not nearly as half-baked as they sound. Tony Robbins seminars have shown me the way (if I can walk on hot coals than I can explore binary star systems on the verge of Type Ia Supernova). Plus, my lawyer informs me, the time is right to make a cosmic statement about the utterly selfish way superior alien races obtain medical data at the expense of our incredibly vulnerable gastrointestinal tract.

In closing, the Klongors endlessly abuse their privileged status in the universe. We cannot allow ourselves to continually be exploited by the scum of deep space! We must insist upon our right to a voice—and not just on *The Maury Povich Show*!

My hope is that we can one day live on a planet as virtuous as the one we visited on the way back from my anal plundering—a magical, rocky land where taciturn jellyfish dominate (so there was no groping, indecent exposure, or secret buttons under desks that trap victims). With your 12 trillion dollar donation—or, hopefully, slightly more—you can help make the space-time continuum a place we are all proud to inhabit!

A Brief Guide To Hell

Welcome to hell! Our only goal here is ruthless torture. If at any point you feel the slightest tinge of enjoyment, notify a whipmaster who will promptly beat the satisfaction right out of you.

Many of you are wondering—at this juncture—if this pit of ghastly flames is really worse than a California Forest Fire? ABSOLUTELY. It's worse than debating Black Lives Matter on Reddit with a gender-neutral cat lady.

That said, because we receive more than 10 million hate letters per day—none of which we reply to (our customer service operators have a lousier temper than Alec Baldwin)—we've provided this brief Q&A (which is really just another excuse to belittle you).

1) It's absurdly hot down here. Make it stop!

You mock nobility, trash the ten commandments, and still feel you deserve central air? Would you also like a Viking sub-zero refrigerator with a no-frost freezer compartment? Face facts—you're doomed.

2) My neighbors won't stop screaming. What is going on?

Platinum-level-sufferers have echo-inducing-torture-chambers that amplify each scream to thunderous decibels. Gold-level-sufferers get beaten by a barbed horse whip till they whine like vegans when the health food store runs out of spirulina. Blue-level-sufferers are disemboweled to the point where they go deaf from listening to their own wretched pleas for help played back for them on an Alexa (Amazon gets tax breaks in hell too). Of course, if you join our Painful Rewards Club Program, hell is even more agonizing.

3) This place is filled with smoke. Yet everywhere I look there is a No Smoking Sign. Why?

The Board of Damnation deemed cigarettes a fire hazard.

4) Cigarettes are a fire hazard? Isn't hell already burning?

Yes. Hell is burning. But Satan is a control-freak. There are no flames in hell his puppet government, The House of Damnation, doesn't pre-approve. The House of Damnation further provides a labyrinthine manual filled with arcane rules more difficult to decipher than a four hour lecture by Jacques Derrida. The goal is to guarantee you choke on smoke for all eternity—but never the Marlboro you desire.

5) This place is considerably smaller than Dante's Inferno. Why?

We sold half our smoldering plantations to The Toll Brothers, who dominate an even more unwieldy real estate empire in heaven than on Earth. They've gutted the torture chambers, purchased air rights, and put up towering condos at half-the price of gated communities in the clouds. They offer angels idyllic amenities such as a hot-as-hell-slime pools (that boil you alive) and gyms featuring The Sisyphus 5000 (you thrust a chained bolder up a hill only to have it roll back onto you). The market for these condos has gone through the stratosphere—a surprising development given that this stratosphere is so goddamn far away.

6) Is there any entertainment down here?

You can watch Amy Schumer's "The Leather Special."

7) Anything else?
We have a lake of fire. When Satan feels like it you go in it.

8) My Samsung Galaxy Note 7 exploded. What's that about?
They do so on Earth as well.

9) No, seriously, why do all cell phones stop working down here?
No service this close to the Earth's core (except for a small chamber within the Ninth Circle Of Hell where Satan his own Wi-Fi router). If you want to send a message, we suggest rubbing a few twigs together to create a smoke signal.

10) What's with all the tanning beds?
Those are burn chambers.

11) How exactly do Burn Chambers work?
You are projected into a torture pit, gripped by metal rods, and electroshocked on the hour. There are three settings: crispy, smoky, and nuclear fireball. It doesn't matter what you request. You always get all three. First, you are made crispy as hell, then you get smoky, and finally you get singed by a nuclear fireball. Some sufferers exit the Burn Chamber with a giant fin piercing through the back of their shirt that makes others cry "shark!"

12) I noticed my whipmaster had a pentagram necklace. Where'd he get it?
Demonic Gifts. Sixth Circle of Hell – right behind the tarantula pits. They also sell scythes, goat heads, and lectures by Wayne Dyer.

13) How come in the elevator ride down here all they played is Taylor Swift?
She's on our payroll. As are Lindsey Graham, Rachel Maddow, and The Dali Lama.

14) Can I ever get out of here?

You can apply for an internal transfer to heaven. There is an application process involving a four-thousand page personal essay, ninety-seven standardized tests, and a routine impalement via Ken Burns documentaries (they will be driven like a stake into your heart until you beg us to make it stop).

15) Where do I sign up?

You need to wait a billion years before you can qualify. Once you qualify, then you can begin the process of waiting in line. Once you wait in line, then you can begin the process of being interviewed. Once you are interviewed, you can begin the process of waiting in another line. Then you will be rejected.

16) A friend told me there are no parties in heaven, yet hell has a terrific nightlife. Accurate?

Yes. In heaven there is one bar, Joy To The World, that serves cups of light (i.e. it's less happening than an A.A Meeting). Hell, though, has a lively scene that can best be compared to Mardi Gras. True the fireball shots give you instant throat cancer, and when you throw beads at young ladies they castrate you—but, all in all, it gets better Yelp Reviews than 'Eternal Paradise.'

17) Does hell really have S&M clubs?

Absolutely. Dozens of them. Of course, regardless of preference, you will be the gimp. But this was always your fate, wasn't it? Might as well get freaky, and, against all odds, at least marginally enjoy it.

Brutally Honest Marketing Copy

Facebook – We've sold your personal information to Cambridge-Analytica, which now knows more about you than your subconscious. Why? Because our company is run by an entitled maniac whose sole objective is world domination.

White Castle – If the criminals loitering outside White Castle don't kill you, our pseudo-meat will. Order a Castle Pack of nine burgers and some fries–through bulletproof glass–and expect to get hauled away in a body bag.

Tom's Of Maine – Desperate for your friends and family to stop visiting? Pray every night that your ex-girlfriend will quit stalking? Then try an organic deodorant guaranteed to keep those in your social circle at least fifty yards away. Thanks to the organic properties of Tom's of Maine (aka its lack of functioning), you'll soon become a bearded, muttering recluse who pays his rent by collecting cans.

San Pellegrino – Sure, it's sparkling. Okay, the aftertaste is decent. But eight dollars for a bottle of water lousier than Canada Dry? Seriously, how classy can a bubbly be that's sold at Wawa? Suckers!

Time Warner Cable – Enjoy paying exorbitant fees for a DVR box that refuses to acknowledge the existence of your remote control? Find it appealing that your cable box freezes for hours at a time while you gnash your teeth and plot the destruction of our galaxy? Act now and we'll throw in internet that doesn't work and a home phone line that ensures you're hounded by idiotic telemarketers that barely speak English. Plus, sign up today and keep your $129.99 rate for a full year—even after you hang yourself. That's right. We won't raise your rates—*even after you're dead*!

Sunny Delight – Nine out of ten porn stars on BDSM sites described Sunny Delight "as exactly like drinking piss." They would know.

CVS – We now insist that all customers ring themselves up. Scan your courtesy card, bag your groceries, and then thank yourself for being a valuable unpaid employee. Next we're gonna have you redo our plumbing! Why? Because our only competition is godforsaken Duane Reade!

Uber – All customers get to ride in vehicles operated by a totally unregulated drivers who most often are complete sociopaths. That's right. You'll be paying top dollar to risk getting kidnapped, sodomized, and dismembered. Is Uber otherwise safe? No. If the driver doesn't murder you the way he races the wrong way down a one way street while adjusting his GPS might. And for those who think a negative review will preclude maniacal behavior… please! Deranged lunatics can withstand negative feedback on a digital interface no one reads.

EarthLink – Your free email account comes with the lousiest security features imaginable. Expect daily subjugation to hackers who distribute endless penis-enlargement ads to all your contacts. When you call EarthLink to complain, rude customer service reps will run through the same forty-six steps they follow in all situations. After completing this tedious process they'll hang up on you. You'll call back, endure the same six hour ordeal, only to be hung up on once again. You'll call once more, threatening to murder every last employee in their Bombay office, tying your phone card around your neck, and bashing your printer with a baseball bat before punching yourself repeatedly in the nuts. Next they will tell you there is nothing they can do. And you thought Gmail sucked!

Tabasco-Spiced Slim Jims – Tired of the lean, grass-fed beef at your local butcher? Feel Peter Luger's doesn't quite match the hype? Then try Tabasco-Spiced Slim Jims, a horrid treat that tastes exactly like moldy shoe leather. This low-grade product will rip up your esophagus, induce a stomach ulcer, and, in all likelihood, cause rapid death via toxic megacolon (you get what you pay for).

A.I.G. – We're an insurance agency that protects against calamity. Yet during the economic meltdown of 2008 we're the ones who needed billions in public funds. If we stand for anything it's hypocrisy!

Chipotle – Our food quality standards keep getting lower. E. coli is rampant. But we can't just poison you for free. Hence, from now on there will be a $1.69 E. coli surcharge. Bon Appétit!

J.C. Penny – We're a legacy business built for a dying mall structure that simply can't compete. Our clothing is perfect for a civil war reenactment. Plus, our customer service is a series of interconnected hate crimes. It's reached the point where we're hoping to sell our

J.C. Penny stores themselves on Amazon.

Costa Cruises – Thought the sinking of *The Titanic* was cool? Long to drown in the company of your peers? Then sail our newest ship, *Costa Magica*, into the bottom of The Mediterranean Sea (on the exact route taken by *The Costa Concordia 2*)! Bon Voyage!

Glorious Casting Notices

Showbiz is hardly all opulent award ceremonies and swag parties in East Hampton. Actors working in the lower rungs of the film and television industry generally find it an excruciating affair. The typical background actor works nineteen hour days trekking back and forth through the snow in the hope of obtaining one of three waivers to get an overpriced SAG-AFTRA card (a pipe dream in itself—since these waivers are harder to obtain than a NYC gun permit). The principal actor, in turn, often spends all his free time auditioning in the hope of getting miserable parts, like Gay Amish Psycho #3, in an I.D. Channel reenactment no one but other Gay Amish Psychos will watch.

With this in mind, I've created the following casting notices that emulate what the struggling actor will find on Breakdown Services Ltd. Proof that I was close to the mark is several actor friends I sent these listings to immediately responded with headshots, reels, dietary preferences, letters from a parole officer, you name it. In sum, new actors need to realize that not all entertainment industry productions are quite as glorious as they sound.

DISFIGURED IN IRAQ
Feature Film
Non-Union
Rate of Pay: None
Usage: Festivals/Internet

SUBMIT ELECTRONICALLY
DEADLINE: 03/04/2019
PLEASE INCLUDE SIZE CARDS

IF POSSIBLE PLEASE SUBMIT ACTOR'S ONLINE DEMO WITH EACH SUBMISSION.

Seeking:

PARAPLEGIC SOLDIER—Male 20-35. REAL PARAPLEGIC SOLDIER needed. No pay. But great exposure (to international film producers, and, of course, in many cases, Islamofascist terrorism).

WOUNDED MUTE FREAK—Male 18-25. THE WOUNDED MUTE FREAK is a soldier critically-injured in battle. Actor MUST have stunt experience and be willing to run across sand dunes as REAL EXPLOSIVES detonate. Actor is unlikely to become WOUNDED or MUTE on set as he will be working with the stunt coordinator to ensure his safety. That said, in the event he becomes a real WOUNDED MUTE FREAK, he may have the opportunity to go from a supporting to a leading role.

BRAIN-DAMAGED, CATATONIC MARINE #1—Male/Female 35-45. THE BRAIN-DAMAGED, CATATONIC MARINE #1 will ideally be a disabled actor who fits the above description. During the audition we will examine all interested parties to ensure sufficient functional-impairment. Those who pretend to be brain-damaged and/or catatonic need not apply. We only have a limited number of audition slots so we are making this crystal clear: *do not even think of applying if you are not severely BRAIN-DAMAGED AND/OR CATATONIC.* Also, NAME ACTORS ONLY. If you don't know what that means don't apply. Further, if you think you are a NAME, but aren't sure you are a NAME, you need to take a blood test to ensure your NAME status meets our standards (this will be certified by Sea Orgs in our affiliate organization, *The Church of Scientology*).

HIPPODROME MADNESS
Short Comedic Film
SAG-AFTRA
Rate of Pay: Deferred (Eternally)
Usage: TBD

SUBMIT ELECTRONICALLY
DEADLINE: 05/02/2019
ACTORS MUST INCLUDE SIZE CARDS

HUMAN CANNONBALL ACT: Seeking a Little Person comfortable being a human cannonball. Actor will be shot out of a cannon at 86 miles per hour before slamming through a table filled with meat pies. (We also intend to have the cast and crew pelt the meat pies at the Little Person as part of the DVD extras). We prefer someone with stunt experience willing to sign a liability waiver (*this is standard protocol given the extreme risks involved*), although we may be willing to accept a particularly gullible amateur. Interested Small Individuals should submit video auditions to diegravitydie@gmail.com. Remember to slate with your name, your height (or lack thereof), and the reason you want to go flying through the air for the cheap laughs it will engender.

DEZI/SASQUATCH– Male/Female 18-55. Dezi is a bearded lady. All types considered. Ideal candidate, though, is a male or trans bodybuilder who looks alluring in a sun dress. Male or trans bodybuilder preferred since individual who plays Dezi will also play the Sasquatch later in the film and must attack random tourists in a menacing fashion (not saying a woman can't do this, but a male or trans bodybuilder with a furry bulge downstairs is ideal). Candidate must also be comfortable strangling CGI chipmunks (real chipmunks will not be murdered unless our laptops crash and we can't operate DaVinci Resolve). Send auditions to hairyandhung@yahoo.com. Remember to slate with your name, your beard length, and the reason you think you have what it takes to play two of the most difficult roles ever invented for no pay in a short that will almost certainly end up rotting in the YouTube graveyard.

MONKEY BOY—Male 10-15 year old. Must be able to cry, spontaneously, at the sight of a plate of fried calamari (a giant squid, Monkey Boy's best friend, abandons him for an orca). In other words, you could say Monkey Boy is easily triggered by calamari and now requires a squid-free-safe-space. Actor should also be comfortable taking enormous quantities of LSD (psychedelics help Monkey Boy realize he is more monkey and less boy). Finally, we need the actor to make himself vomit and then lovingly drink his puke through a straw. Send self-tapes to nastychimps@aol.com.

SLEAZY GATSBY (Extras)
Episodic
SAG-AFTRA & NON-UNION
Rates apply to both Union and Non-Union:
Regular background rate ($152/8) for extras without nudity
Gangbang Victim pays $184/18 hrs plus possible overtime (nudity required)
Gimp #3 pays $192 for Permanent Enslavement

SUBMIT IMMEDIATELY
DEADLINE: 07/04/2019
ACTORS MUST INCLUDE SIZE CARDS

SAG-AFTRA/NON-UNION WOMEN to portray drug-addicted, nympho prostitutes. SHOULD BE COMFORTABLE ENGAGING IN EXPLICIT SEX ACTS (the extent of the sex acts will be determined on set, but all participants must agree to partake in whatever horrors the director has in mind now). All sex scenes will take place at the re-imagined Gatsby Mansion—a kind of voyeuristic spectacle that begins with participants removing flapper dresses and using vintage cigarette holders in surprising ways (not just as sex toys). **Please note you will be paid the regular background rate regardless of what pornographic acts you engage in (this is all our current budgetary restraints allow).**

GANGBANG VICTIM– Blonde female 18-22. Looking for a stunning, well-proportioned actress comfortable playing the victim of forty male assailants—each of whom will be naked but for a top hat and monocle. The angry male assailants will ravage her and then throw her into the street by the neck until she weeps histrionically. Eventually Gatsby will take her in, provide chamomile tea, and violate her as well. Then he will invite all gang bang participants back to his palatial estate in West Egg where they will take turns with her once more. Please note this is a heavily featured role—a truly rare opportunity—and, as such, actual facial features (and not just genitalia) will appear on camera.

GIMP #3—Female 18-19. This is a very unique role. The actress will not just play a gimp who Gatsby chains, beats, and violates in every orifice, she will become one behind the camera as well. The name for your secondary position is Production Assistant.

A STREET CAR NAMED DESIRE
Theater
V/T: Metropolitan Playhouse, NYC
Pay: AEA Showcase ($1.25 Stipend)

SUBMIT TAPES VIA THE CLOUD (not iCloud—Fed Ex Air [aka an actual cloud])
DEADLINE: 09/04/2019

The Obie-Award-winning Metropolitan Playhouse is casting three Equity actors for this innovative theater piece wherein all actors wear poultry costumes.

STANLEY KOWALKSI—A greasy young rooster with burly wings and an angular beak. Muscular roosters who make a ton of noise and are willing to destroy their own coop are best. Additionally, in the climactic scene, the rooster must be willing to lay an egg (never mind if it's scientifically impossible).

STELLA KOWALSKI–A genial, rotund chicken who can't decide whether to support Sister Chicken, Blanche, or her husband, Stanley. By the time she cooks an omelet–made from Stanley's egg–we know she is ready to dismiss Blanche as crazy–and assuage the bitter cries of her rooster husband.

BLANCHE DUBOIS–Prefer deranged actress willing to dress as a giant chicken tender and continually dip herself in honey mustard. Actresses with talent, professional training, and an impressive curriculum vitae need not apply.

ACTING: THE ULTIMATE SCAM
Documentary
Usage: TBD
Rate of Pay: -500

SUBMIT ELECTRONICALLY
DEADLINE: ASAP!

KILL YOURSELF–This is a role as well as advice.

KILL YOURSELF #2–In case you didn't listen the first time…this is your chance.

KILL YOURSELF #3–Stop reading these lousy casting notices. DIE!

CORPSE #1-3–Note To Agents: In case your client took our advice, we are casting corpses ($500 charge to audition–dead or alive).

Jewish Mother Gives The Great Comics Notes

Gilbert Gottfried – Uch! That grating voice! Are you trying to get white nationalists to bring back the pogroms?

Steve Martin – Every time I watch your lousy act I wish the arrow in your head was real!

Bill Maher – Nice cult you got there. I'm just waiting till your lunatic followers start walking on hot coals!

Jim Gaffigan – Dull gentile humor. I don't trust it. You look like a First Commander in the Hitler Youth.

Andy Kaufman – Calling you schizophrenic would be sugar-coating it. You're a moron!

Andrew Dice Clay – No wonder you're in a Woody Allen movie. You two perverted freaks deserve each other!

Carrot Top – Who pays top dollar to see a carrot head? I wanna see a carrot I go to straight to goddamn *Whole Foods*!

Natasha Leggero – You have everything Joan Rivers had *except the talent*.

Jon Lequizamo – Annoying characters rambling on with dopey political messages. Ever heard of a punchline?

Jeff Dunham – If you're the ventriloquist then the audience is your dummy.

Jimmy Fallon – Stop being so friggin' nervous or I'll send you to bed without a baked apple you whiny little putz!

Steven Wright – A shiva call is ten times more lively than your act.

Bill Cosby – You've gotten tons of criticism. But screw everyone. Oops. You already did!

Jackie Mason – Who's your opening act again? Embalming fluid? *Figures*.

Carlos Mencia – Waiter! Mas agua por favor!

Kevin Hart – You happy-go-lucky little troll. Just think of how much better the world would be if your mother had only aborted you!

Imaginary Craigslist Ads

Craigslist is often mistakenly believed to be an amorphous mass of strange queries and madcap pleas for attention. Nonsense! The ads are often spellbinding works of art themselves. Proof of this are the imaginary craigslist ads I created below (which, taken as a whole, clearly deserve the Noble Prize in Literature).

Post#1: Remove Wrecking Ball From Pool And It's Yours

There is a wrecking ball in the bottom of my pool. All summer it has been quite the embarrassment. We try to pass it off as a found object (in line with Duchamp's work), but no one has fallen for our subterfuge. The pool is filthy. Grease and sludge and soot dominate the once pristine waters.

Please, for the love of God, remove this insufferable eyesore. I promise the wrecking ball is yours, gratis, provided you *never bring it back.* It should further be noted that you will need to sign an NDA—as any mention of a Gunite Pool featuring a hideous monstrosity will almost certainly lower the value of our Southampton Estate immeasurably.

Finally, we require a fully-refundable $20,000 deposit. This is necessary insurance against damage to our sculpture garden—that you must traverse, wrecking ball in tow, on the way to driveway. Good luck, and, just so you know, we have an attack dog—a highly-belligerent Rottweiler named Cujo—who incessantly tries to rip every last intruder to shreds.

Post #2: Existential Philosopher Seeks Permanent Temp or Temporary Permanent

Post-structuralists taught that there is a vast difference between "sign" and "signified;" between the word "assistant" and "a living organism who serves this function." Hence, when I say I need an assistant what do I intend? And if I don't know, doesn't this make you even more foolhearted to apply?

Even taking it as a given that you will become my assistant, wouldn't it be a tad impudent to predetermine your length of employment? As Heidegger taught, what matters most is our being-towards-death; our *Dasein*, or presence as it becomes open to truth (Greek *aletheia*); hence, you will no doubt agree to be harassed at times—particularly since neither of us have any real importance in the cosmic scheme?

What is more, there is the problem of accurately classifying your position. Will you be a permanent temp? Temporary permanent? Or some third category that can only be established through a Hegelian dialectic?

Your compensation, too, may never arrive: like Vladimir and Estragon you may never meet this 'Godot.' For the sake of simplicity, though, I can say *it is my intention to pay 12$ an hour* (yet I cannot guarantee it). And, even if payment does arrive, it may feel like 6.00$, perhaps even 2.50$—since I solely pay in rolls of pennies. Then, too, you'll be filtering the digits on your pay stubs through your own distorted solipsistic lens, a hopeless endeavor as David Hume implied when he attacked Descartes' cogito in the philosophical equivalent of The Battle Of

Stalingrad.

Finally, I will provide the highly-reductive list of your daily tasks: faxing, correspondence, email blasts, volunteering as a test subject, and nodding your head while I pontificate. Please note: I am congenial, non-discriminatory, and a strong proponent of worker's rights. Still, when feeling low, I may require you to bow before me ceremoniously while pleading for divine grace.

<u>Post #3: Big Time Scribble Gig</u>

My orange juice went stale before dah goddamn expiration date. I got sick, ended up in dah hospital, and needed to get my stomach pumped.

Now, I don't got no insurance (wise guys don't deal with no pricks from Oxford), so my bill was through dah frekn' roof. I call up dah 1-800 line and dah hoity-toity d-bag refuses to make good on Tropicana's debt. I got a 6k bill here you twat! So I say "pay or I'll pistol-whip yah" and call dah jerkoff a "dick-licking ass monkey." So now…get this…I'm getting sued. *Unfuckingbelievable*!

Anywhooz, I need you to write a complaint letter to Tropicana. You hear me you fanooks? I'm talking to youse!

Job pays forty bucks, veal scaloppini dinner on Mulberry Street, and a free seminar in my basement called *Racketeering 1-2-3.*

<u>Post #4: Hairy Mermaid You Cursed Out At The DMV</u>

I'm the hairy mermaid you cursed out at the DMV. We chatted about Keats, banana bread, and micro-aggressions. Or, rather, I was talking to myself about these topics on a Bluetooth headset so I seemed less insane (ironically, no one was on the other end of the line).

You kept shaking your head till I turned and accidentally struck you with my fish tail. You walked off, shouting angrily about how you "can't stand the stupid fucking rejects at the DMV." Then, in an act of chivalry, you returned, and, under your breath, said "Fish-tits! Back in the aquarium!"

Well, in case you couldn't tell, I found that rant intensely erotic. I'm a sub; highly-obedient; want nothing more than to be your side piece of the sea. Put me in a tank and beat me. Or grill me with rice pilaf and broccoli rabe. *Please*?

<u>Post #5: Crack Den For Rent</u>

Crack Den for rent in lovely Downtown Detroit. The den has old-world charm (built during the war of 1812), the latest appliances (crack pipes), and includes adorable pets (rodent infestation).

The room offers stylized, industrial lighting (a 40 watt bulb tied to a string), a charming backyard oasis (fire pits), and state-of-the-art indoor plumbing (a trash bin filled with slimy excrement).

Be sure to ask about our other units in the same building—most notably a top-of-the-line triplex (garbage chute), with remodeled master bathroom (mechanical room), and a complimentary doorman (vagrant who will open the door for you in exchange for a donation).

All apartments in the building offer luxurious amenities such as dynamic entertainment (fiends stabbing each other), an exercise room (when cops raid the joint you'll feel like you're running on a treadmill), and storage facilities (a shed with rotting corpses). Contact me immediately to move into the best building in the neighborhood (because the others have all been incinerated).

<u>Post 6: Craigslist Parody Writer Needs A Patron</u>

I excel at writing parodies of Craigslist Ads. Unfortunately, there is no money in it. I suppose I could try and get a job writing monologue jokes for late night TV, but I prefer creating humor that has *absolutely no utilitarian function.*

We would not have Beethoven's symphonies without the Archduke Rudolph. Nor would there be transcendent paintings by Botticelli if it wasn't for the Medici family. Anyone want to pay me an obscene amount of money to write Craigslist Ads?

Why the silence? This is my calling! Seriously, I need a patron or I'll blow up a nursery school. No. Forget that. I need a patron or I'll use more chemical weapons on innocent toddlers than Assad! Wait. I thought of something worse. I need a patron or I'll write for BuzzFeed. Come on. Don't you want to save humanity?

The above six posts are proof of the ravishing turns of phrase found in Craigslist Ads. The last post, by the way, I frequently shared on the platform. I never obtained any interest—other than from a foot fetishist who wanted to lick my toes in exchange for providing her a highly-revelatory atv/utv/sno ad. I guess I'm a misunderstood artist. A postmodern Adolf Wölfli. Nothing left to do, I suppose, but retain my good cheer, and, against all odds, carry on.

Confessions Of A Potted Plant

"Weinstein quickly masturbated into the potted plant near the vestibule…" -The Daily Mail

With all the revelations emerging about the film mogul Harvey Weinstein, I'd be remiss if I did not share my own. Me too, friends! Me too! It's not about you…it's about me…too!

Some will say "what right do you have to speak up?" After all you do not even take the human form; a chlorophyll-based Argentinean creature watered three times a week has no place in such a serious discussion! What is more, you're belittling the sexual harassment countless women faced by putting your own plant-based suffering on par with it.

Perhaps. But hear me out! It is not easy to be a potted plant. Relegated to a corner. Ignored. The ultimate afterthought. Many of us die—you heard me *die*—from neglect!

Given these parameters it can perhaps be understood how—for the longest time—I've had severe body image issues. Hailing from Mar De Plata, where the female dieffenbachias tend be more voluptuous, with ponderous, wanton leaves that sag, I've struggled to accept myself as I am—as my plant brethren advised. How I longed for the slender, elegant figure of the orchid! Or the colorful, dynamic persona of the Venus Fly Trap!

I was common. As plebian as a potted plant can be. I in no way impressed and—in full disclosure—had an independence of spirit that made it unlikely I'd ever be taken seriously by the illuminati of film production. It therefore seemed a remarkable stroke of good fortune when I was purchased by Socialista, a favorite haunt of film moguls, and offered the opportunity to dwell among rich velvets and brocades twelve feet beneath a gothic chandelier.

Excited as I was, my insecurities were only magnified by my new genteel surroundings. For I was situated in a row of potted plants far more fetching than I could ever hope to become. They were trim (perhaps having a secret membership at Equinox), with toned leaves, and—from the look of them—turned more carbon dioxide into oxygen than a botanical garden. They were photogenic queens who excelled at photosynthesis! How could I compare?

Night after night I'd watch Mr. Weinstein work subterranean machinations—envious—yes, I said it—*envious*—not so much of the supermodels and starlets he routinely harassed, but of the foliage they were pinned against as he sweet-talked and groped.

Every other plant was featured in a licentious encounter but yours truly! It hurt so badly! Why wasn't I good enough? Did I require the keto diet? Might a bit of pruning help him see the erotic potential in my quirky, corpulent form?

Other plants were objectified and exploited. And? At least they got to star in the backdrop of films like *Chasing Amy* and *Clerks 2!* I was so jealous! What did a dieffenbachia have to do to get felt up by the chairman of The Weinstein Company?

Then it happened. Blessed night! Memory to

crush all others! Lauren Sivan, a charming young journalist, was cornered by the film mogul in the vestibule between kitchen and bathroom.

Not only did Harvey block the door, preventing Sivan from departing, but, as she watched, hissed at her and rubbed his nipples like a Chippendale's dancer. She backed off, her face ashen, when, out of nowhere, he whipped his member out and stroked it fervently.

In under ten seconds he finished in my soil pot, wiping himself on my lovely leaves with a triumphant flourish. That hairy, gorgeous belly. Those pale, grasping hands. The quiet desperation and—moments later—strange pride. It was all so magical!

How the other potted plants shook with jealousy! Every plant in Socialista—indeed, every potted plant in New York heard the story!

It was one thing to have Harvey Weinstein brush up against you. But to complete the ultimate act of Eros inside you? To transform you into the cherished object? *Eureka!* To this day I cannot imagine how he could have selected me over the countless hydrangeas and gloriosas!

And so I am offering this account to *The Huffington Post*—that paragon of factual reporting—not because I want to put Harvey in jail, but because I feel obliged to confess my love for him.

Oh Harv, you and I, plant and beast, should really be reunited like alien and abductee on *The Jerry Springer Show*. I only hope you can seduce me again, and that, soon enough, you will escort me down the red carpet at Cannes. I'll show mad foliage. Be permanent arm candy. I'm docile and willing—exactly what you want from victims and/or spouses (hint, hint). Plus, in a thin, silky red pot, I'm told I look perfectly ravishing.

New Apps

The following apps are in early stages of development.

SHAME CENTER – A competitor of the iPhone's Game Center developed by a Jewish mother.

SNAPBRAT – A Snapchat competitor that scolds the brats who use it.

DATSMACK – A version of Whatsapp that provides free heroin to addicts.

Apps in even earlier stages of development.

CANNIBALY – Spotify for those who eat humans: body parts rotate and you're expected to share.

LINCOLN – Lincoln is like LinkedIn only it connects you to a theater where you will be shot in the head.

GROUPEDIA – A cross between Groupon and Expedia. No one has figured out exactly what that means.

Apps dropped for being too difficult to market.

HERMIT MINGLE – A dating app for hermits that was rejected since hermits don't leave the house.

TUMORTOOTH – An app meant to accompany a Bluetooth-like device embedded into brain tumors. Rejected because the device induced mice to gnaw off their own feet.

SWINGAGO – A Fandango for swingers. Orgy

times, 3D glasses, hot tub bookings, and expert reviews. Rejected because of its similarity to info already conveyed through Backpage.

Apps that will be brought to market 1000 years from now.

GOOGOOGAGA – Get younger every time you sign in.

CASA – Enables you to return home after a long period of time travel (Call The T-Mobile Support Line if you're stuck in a time bubble).

DOPPLEMAPS – Helps locate all your doppelgangers—as many as billions—throughout the galaxy. Find doppelgangers before they find you!

iDICTATOR – Creates new phones, or iSlaves, subservient to the original phone. Face-ID-Assassinations, Hands-Free-Genocides, and App-Based-Chemical-War. The end of humanity available for a small additional fee.

Conversations With Stanley

Since the death of Stanley Kubrick his reputation has continued to soar. Perhaps this is because, in an age of comic-book-fixated superficiality, his work stands out for its methodical precision and satirical depth. Indeed, a whole cottage industry of Kubrick centered media productions has sprung up—museum exhibits, lengthy biographies, even whacko YouTube videos insisting he now works at Chipotle.

While the above is understandable, given his iconoclastic films, I recently witnessed a new low in Kubrick worship—an 81 minute screening of a documentary fixated entirely on the auteur's personal driver. In *S Is For Stanley*, Emilio D' Alessandro describes putting his foot on the gas pedal, and, when the light turns red, hitting the brakes. Yet he was lionized by critics for reasons that remain as mysterious as Bowman's hyperspace journey in *2001: A Space Odyssey*.

It occurred to me, while watching this debacle, that there was but one way left for me to significantly impact the entertainment industry—produce additional documentaries on those who briefly interacted with Stanley Kubrick. Below are excerpts from my forthcoming thirty-six part series, *Conversations With Stanley*.

<u>Sal The Gas Station Attendant</u>

Kubrick pulled up to my gas pump in Sheepshead Bay on a day I'll nevah forget (dat same day I went to dah E.R. after getting half a hot dog stuck down dah wrong pipe). He was a photographer at *Look Magazine* and snapped pics of mwah with his goddamn Rolleiflex. Anywhooz, after the pics, he smirked and goes "fill 'er up." *Genius*! (Even den he knew his car was like a woman—she worked for him, see?).

While I pumped his gas he mentioned it was a cloudy day. I said, "sure is." He goes, "precisely." I go "damn straight." Then he goes "well, it just might rain."

Before he left the future creator of *The Shining* asked what fuel I like best. I got five teeth. Had soot all ovah my ugly mug. Never made it past dah sixth grade. Yet dah greatest director evah wanted to know weder I suggested unleaded or premium? *Holy crapola!*

Last thing Kubrick says to me was "stay outta the rain." *Wowzer!* Ever since, when derz a horrible downpour, I go inside.

<u>Bud The Termite Inspector</u>

On November 12th, 1970, at precisely 4:03 PM, my secretary obtained a cryptic note that read "*Termites! Hurry!*" The envelope contained a return address in Hertfordshire, an area where every last Anglo-Saxon with an even passing interest in cinema knew Kubrick resided. I checked the handwriting against an old signed copy of a Lolita script—that C. Denier Warren had given me after I'd rid him of his cockroach problem—and was shocked to find it a perfect match.

I called C. Denier Warren to confirm, and, sure enough, the home in question belonged to Stanley Kubrick. But how was I to handle his pest problem? Was I really equal to the challenge? After all, opportunities like this come but once in a lifetime.

I found Stanley in his den running lines with Malcolm McDowell. "The scream needs more realism," Stanley was saying. "A man subject to the Ludovico treatment would be truly horrified."

I trembled in my dirt work boots. Few moments in my humdrum existence have compared. I put down my sack filled with Bifenthrin spray, anti-termite foam, and termite-bait packs, and, in an affront to all decency, just gawked.

True, I once took Intro. to Acting at *Shuttleworth College*. But it all seemed so trivial when confronted with the majesty of the great impresario groaning at every last McDowell misstep.

"Mr. Kubrick," I said at last, "I'm here for the termites."

"Yes, yes," he replied, showing me where they had burrowed under the kitchen sink with an employment of technical jargon that rivaled that of a seasoned pest control professional.

"Should be relatively easy to contain," I ventured.

"I trust an Oxford Grad. with an M.S. in Mechanical Engineering has the pedigree to handle it."

I was stunned. Most of my clients could not remember the name of my extermination services company—and it was sewed into the lapel of all our uniforms. This level of familiarity with my operation—in an era where our principal information source was *The Encyclopedia Britannica*—seemed incredibly uncanny.

"I research all prospective employees for as many months as it takes," he added. "You're the best exterminator in a 4000 mile radius."

Needless to say I exterminated his termites with a celerity and passion I normally lacked. My idea was to perform my job with the utmost diligence, and, on the way out, slip him my 8X10 glossy. Admittedly, the maestro hardly was at want for blue-collar types who moonlighted as actors in local theater companies. But what else was a down-on-his-luck exterminator with lofty dreams to do?

Kubrick watched as I began spraying and baiting under the sink before returning to McDowell, who was now bashing himself in the head with his fists. Tears cascaded. Howls echoed with such force the whole estate shook from its foundations. "Try again," Kubrick said. Malcolm made an adjustment and ran the lines once more. Kubrick shook his head in dismay. "Again!"

I finished the job, cleaned up, and handed him an 8X10, mentioning my recent gig playing Barnadine in *Measure For Measure*, and suggesting it would be the honor of a lifetime to audition for any role—however small. He smiled and handed my headshot back to me.

"Not a chance," he said.

"Can I ask why?"

"I saw you performance as Guard #3 in *Julius Caesar*."

"Really?" I was stunned, having forgotten all about that gig at The Jermyn Street Theater.

He smiled, faintly. "My advice is to stick to killing termites."

"So there's no hope for me?"

"Not much. But hey—if you really enjoy it—study at *The Royal Academy Of Dramatic Arts* and one day you might just be slightly less terrible."

These were truly inspirational words. A week later I sold my company and became a full-time student, whom, in less than a decade, was homeless.

Ever since I've bathed in The Thames. Dined on refuse. Juggled soup cans in Kensington. None of this would have been possible without Stanley making me feel so lousy about myself I just had to prove him wrong. Today I'm starving to death—and loving every minute of it!

<u>Margaret The Colon Hydrotherapist</u>

I was just finishing up a session with Gwyneth Paltrow—a regular—when I got a call from an unlisted number.

"Wanna empty a colon?" a dark, mysterious voice mumbled.

"No availabilities today," I parried back. After all I had Richard Branson coming in at 2:00, Sir Paul McCartney at 3:00, and Princess Diana at 3:45.

"It's the auteur," he added.

"Excuse me?" I queried.

"You heard me Margaret," he shot back.

"I don't have time for this," I replied, for I was beginning to suspect this was a prank call from yet another loutish drunk.

"It's S.K.," he whispered faintly.

"Come again?"

I could hear him kick a table.

"Stanley Kubrick!" he said as if tortured by the revelation.

"*Is this another prank*?"

"Lady no. I'm all backed up and need assistance."

The voice was unmistakable. It *had* to be him.

"I'm terribly sorry Stanley. I didn't think it was really you. Tell you what, I'll reschedule Richard Branson and squeeze you in before Sir Paul McCartney."

There was a dial tone and ten minutes later a knock at the front door. I sent the appointment I was treating home—a c-list celebrity with a bit part in a Manson family documentary—rescheduled Richard Branson, and wiped down the exam table just as Kubrick sat down with those shifty, inquisitive eyes.

Thick beard, green army jacket, stifling sense of importance....it was unmistakably the master himself!

Kubrick explained he was about to commence

shooting *Full Metal Jacket* at an abandoned gas works in Leicester and didn't want to take many bathroom breaks. He felt it prudent to empty his colon now.

"I'm having 500 palm trees shipped into Leicester," he said. "By the way do you prefer cash or credit?"

"Up to you."

"We're gonna blow that gas works to smithereens. Should I roll over now?"

"Yes. And pull down your pants."

I complimented him on his extensive knowledge on Vietnam—for he was undoubtedly a veritable scholar on the subject—as he revealed a wan buttocks filled with large black hair patches and a sore red sphincter. He groaned a bit as I repeatedly rammed the tube further between his butt cheeks. All in all though he seemed to take the cold feeling of fluid evacuating his colon in stride.

His colon was full of large black misshapen turds, which I quickly removed and placed in a trash bag. As I did so he broke into a hot sweat.

"Is it okay?" he asked.

"Yes. Drink carrot juice and get plenty of rest. You'll be as good as new in three days."

"Three days!"

"You need to take it easy Stanley."

"We're in late pre-production. I haven't slept in weeks."

Kubrick suddenly began to weep. In a kind of panic I hugged him, his bare ass heaving against the thin exam table paper.

"Oh Stanley. It will be okay."

"The pressure is getting to me," he said. "I'm sorry."

"It's fine. Really. This often happens after a cleanse."

Colon Hydrotherapy often elicits visceral reactions from clients. Piers Morgan once drooled all over his wrists. Meryl Streep got nude and mooned pedestrians in Notting Hill. Still, it was stunning to watch Stanley Kubrick—the notoriously cold, distant filmmaker—emit such an operatic display.

His last word to me was "mama," after which he curdled up in a ball and began sucking his thumb. What a regression! And from an analytic thinker who embedded psychoanalytic theories in his work no less! At loss for what to do, exactly, I patted his hair and sang him a lullaby.

Two years later *Full Metal Jacket* came out. I'd like to think that my work contributed in some small way to his subtle critique of the military-industrial complex. In the very least he helped my business grow exponentially, since he told Sydney Pollack and Ingmar Bergman to try my services—even comparing the way Max Ophüls worked his camera to my fluid motion with a colonics tube.

Elsa The Secret Admirer

Every morning I plotted how I could overthrow Christiane Kubrick and have Stanley all to myself. Long, thick beard. Stern, inquisitive eyes. The wild, frumpled hair of a man who'd faked the moon landing!

I couldn't stop fantasizing about Stanley. His power. His rage. His intensity. I wanted him to manhandle me like Paul Mazursky manhandles Virginia Leith in *Fear and Desire.*

For nearly a decade I bombarded the virtuoso with floral bouquets, priceless jewels, and poems written with my own blood. Nights I'd wait outside the gates of Childwickbury, snapping photos of him in the upstairs window reviewing scripts or budget proposals. He always had the intent look on his face of a monk about to achieve enlightenment.

I wanted to spoil all that. Something had to occupy Stanley other than his Napoleon project. The man had a card catalogue with a description of what Napoleon did on every day of his life. I wanted that absurd obsessiveness focused on me! I deserved it! I'd been abused as a child! This was my comeuppance!

Once, I approached him outside the Warner Brothers lot in Leavesden to profess my undying love, but he merely stormed off to yet another meeting. Another time I begged him to violate me in all my orifices—but he just yawned—and switched trains.

Finally, after years without progress, I managed to sneak on set during production of *Barry Lyndon*. Kubrick was filming the fight sequence between Ryan O'Neal and Pat Roach and yelling into his megaphone. I grabbed his glorious waist and kissed his thick, manly beard.

"Cut!" he shouted. Turning to me, he added, "Who the hell is this?"

His handlers grabbed me and Kubrick refocused.

"Ryan, you're too flat. More intensity. Throw your fists!"

"But Stanley," I pleaded as his team struggled to restrain me. "I'd do anything to have your magical cock in my quivering mouth."

"No," Stanley shouted into the megaphone, still ignoring me. O'Neal danced left then right– "Faster. Everyone else cheer. Hurry. It looks fake."

"Oh Stanley! One lick. Please. One lick of your glorious scrotum!"

"I said get this lunatic outta here! Now!" he shouted into the megaphone, at which point I could no longer resist his handlers. They dragged me off while I wept histrionically.

To be scorned! The ultimate afterthought! My life spent in pursuit of a tryst with a genius– and it barely halted his concentration. How small and unworthy I felt! How marginalized! For the first time I understood the cries of the feminist movement. Patriarchal gatekeepers prevent women like me from truly being heard!

All this being said, *Barry Lyndon*, to this day, remains my favorite film. Nothing has Kubrick's essence, nothing oozes his libidinous energy, quite like those final scenes when Barry watches his son Bryan die. Thank you Stanley. You may not have ever made love to me, but, to this day, I climax at the mere thought of your incomparable vision!

Frederick The Part-Time Dentist

I was Stanley's dentist for one improbable visit. This is in 1968—shortly after his regular practitioner mishandled a root canal. Stanley needed a cavity drilled fast—before returning to the set of *2001: A Space Odyssey*.

I started off with a routine cleaning. Lots of plaque. Yellowing bicuspids. Some minor bleeding of the gums. I recommended a Periodontist.

He disliked this advice. But I pressed him and also offered detailed instructions on brushing his teeth in a more efficacious fashion.

"I've read six books on brushing, twelve on flossing," he replied.

"Maybe," I parried back. "But you don't seem to be pressing the brush firmly enough against the gums."

"I'm busy perfecting a new front-screen projection technique for a film about an astronaut that transcends the space-time continuum," he snapped.

"Excuses, excuses."

"The script is being co-written by Arthur C. Clarke, the preeminent science fiction writer of our time."

"Your gingivitis is still horrible."

Eventually, he agreed that, in spite of his impressive filmography, he needed to brush in a more calculated fashion.

I proceeded to drill the cavity that had been giving him such agony. As I did so, I recited a series of chicken-cross-the-road jokes—none of which he found remotely amusing. True, he may have been preoccupied with "The Dawn Of Man" sequence, which, earlier in his visit, he wouldn't shut-up about. Still, he could have at least displayed some minimal appreciation for my lifelong passion.

Hurt that Kubrick was not amused in the slightest—I drilled the cavity a bit more fiercely than necessary. I saw his fist clench into a ball and noticed the beads of sweat form on his quivering forehead. I had him: I was Crassus and he Spartacus up on the cross. Ha! Not so ingenious now, are we Stanley?

"Spit and rinse," I commanded.

He tried, missing the mark; to witness the great aesthete spitting wildly, the drool sliding down his dingy beard turned my whole body into a sponge of delight.

"What gives?" he asked. "You've been drilling this cavity for two infernal hours!"

"Patience Stanley. *Patience*!"

"Patience? You just drilled half my face off you goddamn jackal!"

What an arrogant wanker! He required up to 140 takes for his actors to deliver a scene that reaches his lofty standards. But he expects perfection from his dental practitioner right out of the gate? *The hypocrisy*!

I put the tubes back in his mouth and continued as before. I wasn't drilling near his cavity. Just burrowing a hole in the side of his tooth for the sadistic pleasure it engendered. As I drilled I moved onto a series of borscht belt jokes revolving around a fly in a man's soup. He squirmed and twisted, writhing even (the jokes seemingly as excruciating as the obscene drilling).

After about the four-hundredth stellar punchline, he screamed with a deafening intensity and knocked all my instruments to the ground. He then cursed me and every last one of my descendants and left without paying.

Do I feel guilty about torturing such a visionary artist? Not at all. The egocentric miscreant deserved it!

Marjorie The Amateur Psychic

Every night I dim the lights, illuminate a single candle, and begin my séance. At the height of this transcendent endeavor I remove a Magic 8 ball from my storage closet, dust it off, and converse with Stanley Kubrick.

Why contact him? Because, in my spare time, I'm a truly horrible indie filmmaker. In fact, my first short was such a fiasco that attendees at the premiere, nearly five years ago, continue to send me death threats.

Kubrick is bored in heaven since filmmaking is outlawed in his jurisdiction (they have him working sixty hour weeks in a halo factory).

Perhaps as a means of retaining some connection to his past, he has become my newest afterlife mentor (my former mentor, Charlie Chaplin, was way too into absurdist pratfalls).

Kubrick punches up my scripts so they generate sufficient mystery. We strategize about how to best employ the Steadicam. We discuss filming solely in natural light with a Carl Zeiss Plannar 50mm f/0.7 lens (as he managed so skillfully in *Barry Lyndon*). My films still suck. That said, during my last screening, I am proud to announce I was not pelted with quite so many tomatoes.

Kubrick tells me that, outside of his daily chess game in heaven with George C. Scott (a rivalry that began on the set of *Dr. Strangelove*), our conversations are the most rewarding part of his day. Thank God I've built such a deep, lasting bond with the maestro of cinema. Anyway, that's how I view it. The staff here insists I'm just another paranoid schizophrenic permanently locked up in Bellevue.

A Zagat Guide To Drone Operators

Zagat was founded in 1979 and shortly thereafter became a cultural institution. Although the print version was recently terminated in the U.S., we've decided to revive it overseas with our most practical guide to date: *A Zagat Guide To Drone Operators*.

"Know your enemy," is a timeless biblical adage (Ephesians 6:11). Now the enemy has the chance to intimately grasp the peccadilloes of the soldiers behind our bureaucratic killing machine (for $15.99—or, for those who prefer to barter, two relatively-healthy donkeys).

We believe *Zagat* will be a particularly strong seller near the Afghani-Pakistani border (where *Yelp* is known solely as the sound American P.O.W.'s make after ISIS fighters douse them in gasoline and set them on fire). It also could work well in Iran as a coffee-table book where little is more hip than an Anti-American sentiment. Finally, in the event this book is a hit, we intend to produce a companion survey: *A Zagat Guide To Afghani Funeral Homes.*

Note: [Last names have been redacted for security purposes].

<u>Dave R</u>.:

Dave is a "repressed homosexual" who overcompensates for his effete, carefully-sculpted image by "killing Taliban Mullahs." He writes haikus every morning, his lifelong passion, and yet admits he finds nothing more fulfilling than "operating a phallic-shaped doomsday device," "playing exterminator," and "unleashing holy hell on the enemy."

Dave is married and yet finds no satisfaction from sexual intercourse with his wife. On nights when he visits a Midwestern-themed gay club, "merely to have a look around," he returns to work immediately and strikes the enemy "with the most enormous payload in Afghanistan." Dave admits that he often "imagines the enemy as a butthole" and his remote "as a tongue giving it analingus," but feels "most soldiers have similar homoerotic preoccupations."

Jill P.:

Jill is a "devout Buddhist" with a "lotus-leaf screen saver." She considers showering more than once a month "a toxic extravagance." An accomplished chef, Jill bakes with "grasshopper flour," since it produces "a far lower carbon footprint than other proteins" and because she got tired of subsisting "solely on julienne vegetables with tofu bacon."

Jill entered the U.S. military in an effort to practice "healing-chakra-compassion," but the requirements of the job forced her to settle for "vengeful mass murder." After hitting targets she "meditates for at least an hour," and once, "as a Muslim woman burned" in a "ghastly fireball," she focused so intensely that she convinced herself "the bitch had it coming."

Don P.:

As a kid Don P. was a video game addict. He

joined the military to prove his mettle to his parents. All through childhood they called him "a lard ass" and a "pathetic tard," since he never seemed to "get off the goddamn couch." Operating drones "reconnects him to his youth." It reminds him, in particular, of "locking himself in the attic" and playing *Duck Hunt* "for months without interruption."

Videogaming runs in his family; his uncle Lenny got the high score on a game of Galaga at a bar called *Coconuts* and his Nephew Scott runs a catering company that provides the buffet spread during *Fortnite* competitions in Las Vegas. Don hopes to one day rival this legacy.

He believes if he keeps "playing the terrorist game," he can be known throughout his military base as an "unstoppable digital avatar" savvy enough to "reach bonus rounds." He also hopes to explore "hidden worlds," "defeat evil bosses," "gain extra lives," and kill terrorists "without pathetic cheat codes."

Alfred D.:

Alfred asked his commanding officer to "repaint his drone black," since a white drone "reinforces weapons-based racism." His desires were rebuffed by the generals, but he still raises hell, arguing that "black drones matter." He got in a fight with another drone operator, Biff L. from Nebraska, who insisted "all drones matter." No, Alfred told him, black drones are "systemically-oppressed" and face "institutionalized-racism," which led them to "brawl UFC-cage-match-style" while the enemy "fled to freedom."

Alfred often "strikes fair-skin targets," and, when he gets a direct hit, celebrates vociferously, for there is little he enjoys more than turning enemies "blacker than Usain Bolt." He hopes doing so "will teach evil whitey a lesson," and plans to "keep assassinating cracker ass mofos." Ultimately, he hopes to become "more of a devil than the white devil himself!"

Angela R.:

Angela R., a fourth-wave feminist, became a drone operator to "get revenge on the patriarchal scum," who, all through her childhood, "ignored her histrionic outbursts." By "co-opting the symbols of female oppression" and "weaponizing her radical ideology," she hopes "to terminate female genital mutilation," which she feels "takes place more often in America than it does in the Middle East."

While a dutiful Marine, who obeys her chain of command, her secret objective has always been to "destroy propagators of misogynistic influence." Primary targets include "wife-beating mullahs" and "Trump supporters" who stone their wives to death "for the cheap thrills." She also wouldn't mind "a targeted drone strike" on "certain American men," who "manspread on the subway" in a way she finds "worse than gang rape."

As per Islamofascist territories, Angela doubts there will ever be normalized gender relations. Still, she hopes Muslim women will one day be permitted to wear burkas "made of microfibers," "flirt with kebab vendors," and maybe even "forget to do the dishes."

Her critics suggest "she's wound tight,"

complain she once "smeared goat blood on the male lockers," and are additionally vexed by her frequent threats to "castrate her superior officers."

Jessup Z.:

Jessup Z., an evangelical Christian, "swears before all that is holy," that it's completely incidental that his keyboard fires his drone when he hits 'alt,' and then 'right.' It is also incidental that the code words he uses for enemy strongholds are 'Russian Collusion,' 'Abolish I.C.E.,' and 'Michael Avenatti.'

Jessup supports tolerance for divergent points of view, "except for those Antifa idiots" whom he feels "should get beheaded systematically by the Muslim bigots they defend." He has been labeled an islamophobic misogynist by his peers, which he considers unjust since he has other pastimes besides "blowing up dumb bitches in burkas."

Jessup has been "banned on Twitter, Facebook, Instagram, and Periscope," and yet at work every day he "fires away," in a way that he wishes, just once, "could be directed at George Soros."

Milton D.:

Milton D. is an impostor who borrowed a friend's I.D. and somehow got security clearance. He admits he "is a clueless SJW" who can "barely pull the pin out of a grenade." While against "harming living creatures on principle," Milton feels doing so "takes power back from Roger Stone," whom he feels certain is "a hardcore Nazi."

Milton learned to operate drones "from the Al-

Jazeera Network," which "he watches even more religiously than Don Lemon." He also used "trial and error," accidentally "destroying a statue of Bashar Al-Assad," a tragedy he insists is "on par with Darfur." Today, Milton's "accuracy has improved tremendously," and he only hits the wrong civilians after "a Twitter spat with Gavin McInnes" or when "triggered by one of those god awful Lock Her Up Decals."

As for the future, Milton hopes to "seduce Angela R.," that "enchanting feminist pilot" with "the incredible man-hating manifestos." He made several attempts recently, at which point she handed him an 87 page diatribe begging him to "screw himself repeatedly in the mangina." Milton is currently receiving psychiatric counseling for PTSD (from the derogatory names Angela has called him).

We hope you enjoyed these excerpts from our new guide. Unfortunately, Zagat is struggling. Last year our profits fell exponentially. Sadly, I can no longer afford a staff of forty-six servants in my marble palace in Tunisia.

So would you mind terribly donating to the Save The Zagat Fund? Without your help we'll be unable to supply the enemy key details about the assailants trying to murder them from the comfort of an underground bunker. Thanks!

Sincerely,

Tim Zagat
Founder, The Zagat Survey

A Misanthropic Guide To The Holidays

Thanksgiving—A ridiculous Pilgrim holiday traced back to a 1621 celebration in Plymouth, Massachusetts. Giving thanks for the harvest made sense then; now the only harvest most Americans procure is from the aisles of Costco. Besides, a laborious dinner with annoying relatives is hardly a cause for celebration. Most often the result is a needless political debate that leads to injurious personal attacks and causes the national suicide rate to soar. And you thought World Poetry Day sucked!

Christmas—A festival commemorating the birth of Jesus once seemed a reasonable proposition. Unfortunately, this holiday has become little more than a corporate-generated excuse to boost the bottom line of greedy retailers with soul-sucking products. Throw in the dopey tree, the fat hobo in the Santa suit, and the prosaic camaraderie—all forced down your gullet as if you were a goose bred for foie gras—and you actually might start believing the best thing you ever heard of in your life is a discounted iPod Stereo at shitbag Walmart.

If Jesus ever returns he will immediately check himself into the Betty Ford Clinic. What do Black Friday discounts on a Nintendo Switch have to do with Christmas? And why must I suffer through holiday jingles every year from endless ragtag a cappella groups? Kill yourselves!

Independence Day – In theory this holiday commemorates the liberation of the thirteen colonies from the British Crown. In practice no celebration seems quite so hypocritical. Think about it. We're celebrating the independence of a country that for hundreds of years subjected a whole race of people to legalized slavery. How can we have treated African-Americans as property yet blather on about how we champion liberty and the pursuit of happiness?

Then, too, we boast that our Constitution guarantees inalienable rights when we basically have a two-hundred and thirty year history of trashing and degrading the autonomy of man. Just look at how we've treated the Native Americans (theft of land, rape, genocide etc.), or Japanese-Americans during WWII (hate crimes, internment camps)!

Exacerbating matters further, the NSA violates privacy rights, corporate lobbyists turn our elected officials into pawns, and drones assassinate suspected-enemies without due process in a direct affront to our democratic ideals (which is not even counting all the dead civilians the military counts as 'collateral damage').

So cheer your little fireworks, host a festive barbecue, and lionize our founding fathers when everything America stands for is a lie. We are but cogs in a demented, imperialist machine. Independence Day my ass!

Easter—You already celebrated the birth of Jesus, now you have to make a big tadoo over the resurrection too? When does it end? Should we have a holiday for every last cabinet Jesus assembled while a carpenter in Galilee?

Even more intolerable are the anthropomorphic bunnies bringing children colored eggs. What kind of opium were the German Lutherans smoking when they devised this utterly ludicrous myth? Then there are egg hunts and egg dances, which make one think this isn't a religious holiday so much as an *Alice In Wonderland* reenactment. This year, for Lent, do yourself a favor and give up Easter!

Memorial Day—A holiday intended to honor our fallen soldiers. Sadly, many millennials commemorate this holiday by sharing dick pics with disinterested paramours they superliked on Tinder. Throw in the way millennials ingest Tide Pods now in an effort to be cool, or smoke salvia and then post asinine videos on Periscope, and you have to wonder if all the sacrifices made to protect future generations of Americans were worth it?

Flag Day—A holiday celebrating a piece of cloth with a tag on it that reads "Made In China." What a farce!

Valentine's Day—Saccharine romance. Cheesy flowers. Doltish poetry. Only a lunatic could enjoy such a travesty!

Halloween—It's always a tad nauseating when yet another tween dresses up like Miley Cyrus or Ariana Grande. Throw in the par-for-the-course vampires and ghouls, the playboy bunnies and princesses, and it is surprising that this holiday doesn't drive more gun-toting maniacs into murder-suicide mode.

About the only way Halloween could attract my attention is if a bunch of these repressed soccer moms, who dress in ridiculous, skimpy outfits each year, were simultaneously burned at the stake. Seriously, I'd pay top dollar to see a Joan Of Arc Halloween Spectacular!

SantaCon—An annual pub crawl where everyone dresses up like Santa. In case it isn't painfully obvious, the overwhelming majority of these pseudo-Santas badly need to check into a Phoenix House. It certainly beats puking green vomit all night in an alley.

Santa Con cheapens the myth behind an exalted Christmas figure while driving the sober members of society absolutely nuts. *Another Santa*? *Another one?* I find myself saying this with greater incredulity every year.

I don't believe in the Bible. But I sometimes wish a merciful God would create another flood to destroy the dregs of humanity. Why must these buffoons torture the rest of us with such horrid impunity?

Columbus Day—Don't get me started!

Rejection Letters For Famous Authors

It is fortunate that the great authors of antiquity are not alive today. If so we might never have heard of them. Below are samples of the rejection letters they might have received given our current, dismal literary market.

<u>The Catcher In The Rye</u>

Dear J.D. Salinger,

We very much appreciated reading your non-fiction book about a down-on-his-luck baseball player lost on a cornfield. Even though this narrative isn't right for us—since we exclusively publish bildungsroman's featuring cynical boarding school dropouts—we thank you for the opportunity to consider your work.

Sincerely,

John B. Riley
Assistant To The Assistant Editor, Random House

<u>The Sun Also Rises</u>

Dear Mr. Hemmingway,

We are very grateful for the opportunity to read your ambitious, insightful novel. Unfortunately it does not meet our needs at this time. Since you asked for feedback, might we suggest you make this slightly less depressing? We understand the cyclical nature of drinks and dull conversation is intended as a realistic portrait of the ex-pat circles in Paris post-WWI, but we still feel the novel needs a shocking climactic twist à la a James Patterson novel.

One option would be to have Brett shoot Jake in the face, Robert Cohen punch out Brett, and then have the bullfighter finish them all off with his sword as Mike looks on and chuckles while the sun also rises.

Best of luck!

Archie Nielson,
Intern, Penguin Group

<u>The Stranger</u>

Dear Mr. Camus,

May we suggest psychological counseling?

The Editors

<u>Ulysses</u>

Dear Mr. Joyce,

Are you on IG? How many Twitter followers do you have? Would you be willing to fake your own death to boost sales?

While this book isn't right for us, we need

someone to write a teen vampire saga in the style of *Twilight*. Help us corner the YA market and we'll consider turning *Ulysses* into a made-for-tv movie.

As for *Ulysses's* prospects as a stand-alone novel, again, our deepest regrets, but it has far too much merit to ever seriously consider it.

Peter Brooke,
The Vile Human Being Literary Agency

Lady Chatterley's Lover

Dear Mr. D.H. Lawrence,

We regret to inform you that we will be unable to consider *Lady Chatterley's Lover* for publication without a drastic rewrite. It is our belief that this narrative needs more sensational romantic encounters (ideally revolving around a paddle, a pair of handcuffs, and a ball gag).

While the quality of your writing is undeniable, the sex scenes between Lady Chatterley and the gamekeeper seem far too prudish by today's standards. Nor are they sufficiently frequent. We suggest you reread the *50 Shades of Grey* trilogy and cut and paste where appropriate.

Sincerely,

James Bismutty
The Hot Nipple Press

Waiting For Godot

Dear Mr. Beckett,

Dull characters. Zero plot. Lousy dialogue. Please reread Aristotle.

Sincerely,

Robert McKee
Screenwriting Coach/Producer

Macbeth

Dear Mr. Shakespeare,

We really think this would work better as a high-concept romantic comedy.

Best,

Ben Stiller
Actor/Producer/Development Exec.

The New Testament

Dear Twelve Apostles,

While we appreciated your very dramatic renderings of the story of Jesus H. Christ, we regret to inform you that we can only publish one of your testimonies. We suggest all of you go home, revise your holy scriptures, and resend them to us with a $45 reading fee and a statement about what you will do with the $12.57 in royalties in the unlikely event you actually get published.

Sincerely,

Jim Search
The Lakewood Church Bible Group

A Tale Of Two Cities

Dear Mr. Dickens,

We'll publish this, but only if you make it a tale about one city. And that city has to be Cleveland.

Kindly Yours,

The Editors

Ancient Hieroglyphs

Dear Egyptian Slaves,

We are sorry to report that we cannot publish your excellent hieroglyphs. Market conditions are tough and we cannot make sense of these ornate symbols—even with the Rosetta Stone. But we encourage you to keep engraving your ancient psychobabble into everything from a tomb to a sphinx in the hope that they'll one day end up in The Metropolitan Museum of Art.

Best,

Pharaoh

Four Hot Stock Picks From Satanwater Destructive Capital

Luce F. R. founded Satanwater Destructive Capital shortly after he realized investing in repugnant companies is often highly profitable. The investment firm serves a wide range of felonious clients almost certain to spend eternity in hell. It also manages the wealth of central banks and foreign governments—helping them—wherever possible—fund terrorist activity.

S.D.C. applies a global pitchfork investing approach. New investment opportunities are located by peering into the souls of the doomed. The hedge fund returned as much as 666% last year—including capital gains taxes it never paid.

Here are Luce F.R.'s largest positions and the reasons his firm is likely to continually produce outsized returns.

<u>Envirusment (ENV)</u>

Envirusment is the fourth largest position in the SDC portfolio. The company acts like a virus in the environment, dumping toxic chemicals into rivers, engaging in large-scale deforestation, and burning billions of tons of fossil fuel. Its products and services have completely destroyed the Bosawas Biosphere Reserve, polluted Glacier Bay, Alaska, and expedited the melting of the polar caps. Analysts have pegged ENV's growth of evil rate at an average of a googolplex per year, although that number may soon rise (they are hoping melting the Ozone will help). Former fund managers Jeffrey Skilling and Raj Rajaratnam have not only invested heavily in ENV, but, from the confines of jail, are negotiating deals to become corporate sponsors.

Profit From Killing Helpless Civilians (PFKHC)

Profit From Killing Helpless Civilians is the twelfth largest position in SDC's portfolio. Wait. My bad. They just killed the statistician. They are the now third largest position in the SDC portfolio.

PFKHC manufactures, licenses, and distributes defense technology specifically-designed to assassinate the innocent: Nursery-School-Targeted PAC-3 Missiles (NSTPAC-3), CUL8TR Bystander Drones (CUL8TRBD's); Big Brother Assassination-Targeting Surveillance Systems (BBATSS); Church-Detonating Intercontinental Ballistic Missiles (CDICBM's), and the B87, a variable-yield nuclear gravity bomb that is routinely tested on its own employees.

In order to boost EPS in the coming quarter it has recently considered innovative strategies such as selling its entire catalogue of highly-lethal weaponry directly to Iran. ISIS, in fact, intends to use this technology in their next promotional video—as they feel it will be an even better recruitment technique than routine beheadings.

PFKHC pays a dividend of 14.7 % (on a murder of innocents ratio of 82%). This trounces the company's peers Lockheed Martin and The North Korean Government, which yield 5% and indentured servitude to The Supreme Leader of North Korea respectively (on a meager 14% murder of innocents ratio).

On the horizon for PFKHC is a new version of the suitcase nuclear bomb, tentatively titled the "toothbrush nuke." Colgate hopes to sell it at Duane Reade. The ghosts of Muammar Gaddafi and Osama Bin Laden are huge fans of the stock.

International Youth Exploitation Partners (IYEP)

Luce F. R. increased his stake in International Youth Exploitation Partners last quarter. It is now SDC's second largest position.

IYEP exploits labor laws, poverty in indigenous zones, and the U.S. position of global dominance to provide a highly productive army of child slaves. IYEP has a market cap of 12 billion, which is also the number of children it puts to work in poorly-ventilated coal mines.

IYEP hopes to continue to grow corporate profitability by implementing such efficiency-improving strategies as public whippings, the elimination of bathroom breaks, and amputation of slothful limbs.

Goldman Sachs recently boosted its rating on the company to "strong buy." They laud IYEP's "impressive track record in El Salvador" and its "commitment to autocratic indoctrination." Other analysts forecast that IYEP will expand its EPS at an average rate of 12% per year, largely through the periodic whackings of Human Rights and S.E.C. officials. Dennis Kozlowski, the former C.E.O. of Tyco, is a major investor in the company.

Fleece Your Own Corporation Incorporated (FYOCI)

Fleece Your Own Corporation Incorporated is the largest position in SDC's portfolio. It was created so that those in the C-Suite and on the board—among them Luce F. R.—can profit from the fools working beneath them. FYOCI is a generator of neatly packaged lies, thoughtful manipulations, and a highly-sophisticated bonus structure that funnels all profits to the top.

The company had a market cap of 476 billion, but yesterday the C.E.O. spent it all on a vacation to Tahiti. Analysts predict EPS will only rise if its engineers devise a new line of products that successfully screw the consumer—Plasma TV's that melt, self-driving cars that flee their owners, planes incapable of leaving the runway etc.

One Credit-Suisse analyst predicts this will occur at a 47% growth rate, largely because he gets kickbacks from the executives at FYOCI. Another analyst committed suicide rather than admit FYOCI was the next Lehman Brothers. FYOCI is owned by Angelo Mozilo, former C.E.O. of Countrywide, and is considered a major winner by Bernie Madoff, whom, as everyone knows, made a fortune fleecing his own horribly phony corporation.

Disclosure: I have no positions in any stocks mentioned and no plans to initiate any in the next few lifetimes.

In Defense of Sorority Slang

Throngs of bibliophiles, parents, and scholars alike bemoan the proliferation of sorority slang. It's indoctrinated our youth. Led to laziness and imprecision. Shackled our diction with an air of unreliability.

Or so the argument goes. For while I am not a huge fan of sorority mixers, alcohol poisoning, or Spanx, the critics seem a tad presumptuous. Sorority slang needs to be exonerated, particularly by the literati, who could improve their diction by employing it. Below I identify several aspects of sorority slang in an effort to highlight its daily usefulness and mellifluous potency.

<u>The Poetry Of Like</u>—Many of us use like solely as a verb or a preposition. This is utterly provincial. Would Shakespeare, who invented 10,000 words, so wholeheartedly shackle his own grammatical exploration? It is a lack of imagination that bars us from using like as a noun (I gotta go to the *like*…) an adjective (he's like *like*…), and the beginning, middle, and end of a sentence (*Like like like*!)

Shakespeare famously stated "brevity is the soul of wit." If this is accurate then sorority sisters are linguistic trailblazers worthy of being mentioned in the same sentence as E.E. Cummings. For sorority sisters transmit meaning without the need for an unnecessary level of antiquarian comprehensibility.

Besides, the almost mystical alliteration lifts sorority slang above more plebian forms of dialect. Even Edgar Allen Poe, who began *The Raven* "once upon a midnight dreary, while I pondered weak and weary," does not fully match the operatic effect produced by cackling sorority sisters hovering like vultures over the display case at David Yurman Jewelry.

The Epistemological Brilliance of You Know—Sorority sisters are uniquely perspicacious about the way knowledge is burdened by postmodern self-reflexiveness. This explains why they rarely finish a sentence without remarking, "you know?" Improbable as it may seem, these Tinder-addicted, hair-twirling sages are at the cutting edge of the quest for enlightenment.

Reality is in flux. Quantum Theory teaches us that the fundamentals of physics are far more unpredictable than Newton imagined. M-theory posits our universe may be but one membrane in an infinite sea of universes. With this kind of uncertainty, and grounded, eternal knowledge a pipe dream, it seems inordinately astute of sorority sisters to require epistemological confirmation of every last uncensored thought.

Sure if Strunk and White visited a typical sorority mixer today, with the chewing of green bubble gum, inhalation of copious wine coolers, and the overreliance on *you know*, they might have a seizure. But this is an antediluvian perspective.

That constant reference to the other, that search for confirmation, that challenge to the principles of solipsism place sorority sisters at the cutting edge of twenty-first century philosophical thought. *They know that you need to know that they know.* What?...I'm not sure...but they want to make sure *you know it*, and right now, completely, *you know*?

The Exuberance of Super—The sorority sister reliance on *super* is a revolutionary linguistic choice. Ours is an age of negativity. Think of great modernist works like T.S. Eliot's *The Wasteland* and Hemmingway's *The Sun Also Rises*. Too often artists fixate on a dearth, a meteor crater of limitations.

In marked contrast sorority lingo emphasizes abundance. Consider one sorority sister whom I heard declare, "he's like *super sweet*, and, you know, *super super cute*." Certainly, our great literary minds cannot equally describe the unheralded potential of a frat boy suitor with a flat top haircut. Plus, such lingo is even more effective than the techniques in *Cosmo* at getting your new boy toy to pay for an unlimited supply of Long Island Ice Teas.

Some find the regular use of *super* a sign of impaired mental acuity, but viewed from an alternate lens it could be considered immensely creative. For repetition is often a sublime poetic device, highlighting meaning in ways otherwise impossible. Indeed, repetition is a key motif in a memorable work like Robert Frost's "Stopping By Woods On A Snowy Evening." Sorority sisters are no less skillful. Let us honor them for an unparalleled rhythmic ear and masterful syntactical dexterity.

The Mysticism of Whatever—*Whatever* is perhaps the most pithy way to end a conversation. Sorority girls often use it after obtaining harrowing news (such as an H.P.V. diagnosis). The mysticism here comes from a monumental insight into our helplessness before the crushing randomness of an indifferent universe. When a sorority girl says *whatever* she is really partaking in Buddhist-style non-attachment. This self-abnegation frees her from untold sorrows, and, in certain cases, elevates her to a demigod.

One sorority sister I know learned she had leukemia, adjusted her push-up bra, started a FB Live Video (so the Oncologist could restate her diagnosis), and then went *whatever* with such aplomb her video immediately obtained 6 million views. She then returned to blow-drying her hair.

<u>The Immediacy of I'm Horny</u>—Too often we fixate on political and intellectual concerns without regard for the desires of the body. Sorority girls reorder this societal paradigm. The use of *I'm horny* at a cocktail party can shake up a stultified atmosphere.

I experienced this phenomena last week when my wife, a former Sigma Delta Tau, whispered *I'm horny* into my ear while I chatted with the Chancellor at Brandeis. I blushed. There was an awkward moment. Shortly thereafter, my wife and I excused ourselves and engaged in a dynamic repartee on the merits of the karma sutra.

Before long I grabbed her by the hair and threw her in the bathroom where I drilled her like a Transocean oil rig seeking black gold. The chancellor walked in on us. If I remember correctly, his response was *whatever.* I guess all the sorority girls he dated while running Brandeis influenced him—for no other comment could have been as pithy.

In closing, sorority slang should be made into our national diction. Let us stop relying on ornate Anglo-Saxon words and return to the type of party girl vernacular that can help our species reach the height of collective brilliance. Plus, when you employ a specialized diction you repeat yourself incessantly, which is highly ergonomic.

It might further be advantageous for us all to attend frat parties where sorority sisters get together on stage, cackle, take selfies, and congratulate themselves on being superstars. For each off handed-comment, each outburst in a nasal voice, each act of verbal defiance is invariably more profound than anything in the Bhagavad-Gita.

I'd love to explain further. But it's best to think like a sorority girl. And so *like*, *you know*, my wife's *super horny* now, so if *you know*, you *like* don't agree, *like like die.* I mean it.... *like* die. And if you don't wanna die, *like whatever*, just, *like*, *you know*, leave me alone, you *like like whatever; I'm horny oh my gawd,* sooo *super like* yes *whatever, super horny–like horny*, *horny*, *HORNY–whatever,* oh my gawd, *like, you know*?

Instead Of My Memoir

Memoirs today are filled with corny plotlines, dopey characters, and narcissistic bilge. And, in saying this, I am referring to the more accomplished titles.

Below I summarize four key types of memoirs—largely as a way of talking myself out of writing my own (honestly, I'm more stimulated by the prospect of watching reruns of *Lou Dobbs Tonight*).

Woe Is Me Memoir

The *Woe Is Me Memoir* portrays minor inconveniences as Elizabethan tragedies. While the writers of these works occasionally provide noteworthy insights, it is hard to ignore the violin frequently roaring in the backdrop.

Memories of Growing Up Poor In Beverly Hills is a noteworthy example. Not only was the author, Hanna Wilshire, awarded a residency at *The Breadloaf Writer's Conference*, she was mentored by the ghost writer for Snooki's novel *A Shore Thing*.

This tutelage has had, at best, mixed results. For while at moments her prose achieved remarkable gravitas, at others she drowns in luxuriant self-pity.

On page 6 Hanna states:

> *In those days we suffered unthinkable horrors. Afternoons we scavenged through the fridge for leftovers: plebian 2lb lobster tails, run-of-the-mill steak tar-*

tar, despicable Nobu sushi. That year Daddy failed to earn a bonus bigger than Texas's G.D.P. Mother told us not to worry; we tried, difficult as it was, to remain defiant—until we were late on our country club dues.

Mother went into a tizzy. Soon we were dropped from golf to tennis members. I could hardly order my ball boy around without my friend Priscilla decrying me "a broke ass thot."

Most tragic of all was Daddy's sweet sixteen gift: a Tiffany's silver brooch. To think he couldn't afford Cartier!

Hanna writes with remarkable candor about her struggles as an elitist prep school kid mired in privilege. Yet she seems unable to escape her bubble. By page 579 identifying with her plight seems about as likely as the theory that Planet X is on a collision course with Earth.

We eventually sold our Aston Martin and purchased a Ford Mustang. When my classmates at The Harvard-Westlake School learned what Daddy was driving they sent me a gift certificate to J.C. Penny—the ultimate insult.

I was seriously contemplating suicide when Daddy replaced the Mustang with a Rolls-Royce. I tried to smile, but all that came out was tears. It was too late. The damage had already been done.

An investment in Amazon and some real estate purchases in The Silver Lake area restored the family's fortune—a horribly unsatisfying ending given all the whining that preceded it.

Freaky Childhood

The *Freaky Childhood Memoir* takes place in a small town filled with weird locals embroiled in preposterous circumstances. The authors of these memoirs are generally sufficiently insightful. The problem is these tales strain credulity.

One example is *Lunatic Dreams In Los Alamos*, Fred Outlanda's bizarre account of the side effects of growing up next to a nuclear testing site. Outlanda is brave to discuss how his family suffered. Still, the side effects they endured during the 1950's seem embellished to the point where I might as well have been reading a Phillip K. Dick novel.

In Chapter 5 Outlanda states:

> *The last round of nuclear testing was most dramatic. The house keeled over. Plates shook. Our chandelier shattered. Still, government officials told us not to worry.*
>
> *They were wrong. A week later mom grew a kangaroo pouch. Dad had a shark fin. My brothers and I each developed octopus tentacles. Our chocolate lab had it the worst though: radiation transformed him into an overweight parakeet.*

While living in proximity to Los Alamos, might, in theory, cause physical deformation, I severely doubt the author's mother grew a kangaroo pouch. And a father with a shark fin!

Please! It sounds like the basis for a weird sequel to *Finding Nemo*!

But even supposing a degree of creative license, what happened next seems less plausible than the theory that corporations are fluoridating our water supply as a means of disposing of industrial waste. Outlanda and his family were supposedly taking a hot-air balloon ride in Roswell, New Mexico when they were captured by the U.S. Air Force and imprisoned in Area 51. Outlanda states:

> *We looked so strange—my sister hairier than a Sasquatch—the rest of us with extra appendages—that the Air Force mistook us for aliens. In fact, the classified program "Mogul," featuring a high-altitude service balloon the government used to explain the U.F.O. crash in Roswell in 1947, was really just our family going on a joy ride.*
>
> *Even zanier, though, than the way we were tortured, prodded, and operated on by overzealous scientists, was the time I wrapped my octopus tentacle around the researcher Zelda Markowitz until she became smitten. Not only did we marry; upon my release, our three kids, each with octopus tentacles, became a testament to the idea that love can flourish in spite of radiation poisoning.*
>
> *Amazingly, our oldest son, who resembles a giant squid-headed alien, is now an actor in B-movies—potentially because he routinely saves production tens of thousands of dollars in SFX.*

In the end Outlanda gets abducted, explores The Sunflower Galaxy, and returns to his couch a defeated man. Anyway, that's how he describes it. His wife believes he invented this final ordeal after spending too many nights eating mescaline while listening to *Coast To Coast AM.*

Learning Experience

In learning experience memoirs the writer explores personal insights so exhaustively that it becomes sickening. The goal is to convince the reader there must be some remotely profound element amongst all this bilge.

The other key element is the way arcane knowledge is sui generis in such works on topics like woodworking, game theory, and karmic breathing. A good example of all this is *Masturbatopia*, Archie Lemon's account of his addiction to internet porn.

Lemon describes growing up on a farm in Wells, Maine where there was little to do but grow corn, tend animals, and, when lonely, jerk off. He often uses the phrase "choking his chicken," which, at one point, serves as a rather strange lead-in to a six page treatise on the deleterious effects of the factory farm industry.

While I laud Lemon's innovative structure (each chapter concludes with a strange, kinky fantasy), the learning experience that follows these sessions is rarely noteworthy. On page 87, Lemon writes:

> *I couldn't resist another night of self-love to HD videos of Latina housemaids. Man strives for some higher ambition or is*

brought down by his own devices. Always, I returned to my own self-indulgent nature (and my tendency to choke my chicken so forcefully that my shaft formed scab-like sores).

And on page 292 he adds:

> *Finally, I found Sex Addicts Anonymous. They helped me replace porn with stupid cat trick videos. They also convinced me to wear a robotic lock and load chastity device that literally saved me from a potentially lethal genital infection. By the grace of God I stopped thinking about sex long enough to secure a job at a homeless shelter. The greatest pleasure I've had since is from making a difference!*

While I laud the way Lemon grapples with a taboo subject in graphic detail, the hokey learning experience seems tacked on. Even stranger, though, is the way he begins lecturing the reader, on page 431, on the virtues of a gluten-free diet:

> *Gluten is a gelatin substance made of eight compounds the body cannot break down. It is a composite of storage proteins called prolamins and glutelins. It gives dough its elasticity and can trigger adverse auto-immune reactions.*
>
> *I learned, later in life, that gluten is demonic. If you want an exorcism eat gluten. As for me, once I cut it out, I was reborn!*

Lemon goes on a series of seemingly random

tangents for another two-hundred pages. Then there is an Intermission, or, as he calls it, a Masturbation Break. Only suicidals who lack the inner temerity to finish themselves off should consider reading this book.

Depressing Celebrity Nightmares

Depressing Celebrity Nightmares are most often written by aging rock stars, washed up game show hosts, and melancholy porn stars. The goal is a career jolt. Unfortunately, in most cases, the career is in such shambles that even disgusting sensationalism cannot save it.

What is more, many of these memoirs are packaged as presenting a deep, probing analysis, when, sadly, the most revealing aspects are generally absurdist harangues excerpted from a defunct Twitter feed.

A telling example is *Ninja Pajamas*. The author, Nick Growis, is a retired porn star who went on to voice several animated characters in films like *Shrek 2* and *The Lion King* (he applied himself to V.O. work like a ninja and always loved pajamas—hence the title).

The critical focus of the memoir is the way Nick was wrongfully brought up on murder charges (after police found his wife's mutilated body in a bowling alley). Nick spent six years in prison prior to being vindicated by DNA evidence. Still, even if Nick never committed murder, he confesses, in rather unflinching terms, to severely beating his wife with a spatula. He writes:

I hated that two-bit whore. Every night I smacked her in the head with a spatula. Problem was I wasn't enough of a maniac to finish her off with my .45. Still, after they found her disfigured body behind the AMC bowling alley pins I did six years in San Quentin.

I'm no saint. Ashamed to admit this, but, truth be told, I once shoulderblasted her right in the goddamn mouth! Still, I swear on my mother's grave I didn't kill that hussy! Why would I? She wasn't worth it! Her sister—her sister I could have beaten to death and then sold the recording as a snuff film. But not her!

Work like this is often published simply because the editor figures celebrity status will give the author a pass. Indeed, celebrities have literally written "blah blah blah sex….blah blah blah I'm crazy," and obtained a Harper-Collins contract. By the end of the memoir Growis seems resentful:

Six years in the pen. I took it up the rear till I couldn't see straight. One night it was a long line of Neo-Nazis with pathetic grins. Another night the members of The Muslim Brotherhood took turns until I prayed to Mecca. My rectum would fall out my behind—I'd put it back—and it would fall out again—so that I couldn't help but weep at these hopeless state of affairs.

When I finally got out, first thing I did was hire a hooker and punch her in the nose. This was a terrific stress relief—and way more exciting than watching Connor get beatdown by Khabib on UFC.

I then murdered a random homeless guy. It was even more enjoyable.

Unfortunately, ever since I've been back in the pen—and all the inmates have been taking turns on my backside. My rectum is like a silo for inmate jizz. Plus, I have AIDS and Hep. C. I guess being a famous entertainer isn't all it's cracked up to be.

Employ this memoir as kindling. Unfortunately, even then, it's unlikely to retain any value.

Conclusion

I by no means seek to discourage the penning of future memoirs. Just be wary of the vexing nature of these works, the collapse of publishing, and the fact that no sane individual could possibly want to read another formulaic cry for help.

Roasts Gone Bonkers!!!

Nearly every comedian has faced a room where he falters and cannot win back the crowd. Yet the roast is unique because it offers comedians the opportunity to truly drive a crowd apoplectic. Unfortunately, I seem to be a master at the above. Here are accounts of four roasts from my fourteen year career.

The Roast of Mrs. Piggy

A large gala filled with Muppets dressed in tuxedos and ballroom gowns heavy on frills, lace and flowers. Began by taking a few stabs at Kermit, Crazy Harry, and the Great Gonzo. Soon I went in for the jugular by deriding Henson's early creation, Rowlf, a piano-playing anthropomorphic dog. Howls of protest followed from the back of the room that I recognized, instantly, were voiced by Bert and Ernie.

Of course I suggested Bert spend a few weeks fondling Ernie's rubber ducky, a nice pun, I thought, since Sesame Street writer Mark Saltzman had recently implied the two of them were gay.

Unfortunately, as there were many left-leaning Muppets in the crowd, my politically-incorrect joke got more howls of disapproval. Sensing impending doom, I quickly recovered by praising Big Bird's yellow bonnet as well as making obscure references to the incredible classiness of Gonzo's main squeeze, Camilla The Chicken.

Next I really got in trouble. Having settled the crowd, I decided to mock the Cookie Monster by beating myself until blue in the face and singing, "F is for Fatty, So Planet Fitness Is Not For Me!"

Soon Timmy Monster, Thog, and Sweetums became so incensed that I would parody a creature who was already a parody that they charged the stage. Bedlam followed: nearly seventy-five Muppets from Sesame Street, The Muppet Show, Fraggle Rock and Muppet Babies assaulted me in a dreadful rage.

If it weren't for Oscar the Grouch and Yoda, who calmed the crowd by doing impressions of each other, I am fairly certain I wouldn't have survived. The roast ended by me stabbing Mrs. Piggy, putting her on a spittle, and serving her up to the group as a peace offering.

The Roast of Kenny Rogers

After listening to The Roast of Miss Piggy on *National Public Radio*, Greg Oswald, Kenny Rogers's agent at William Morris, contacted me to partake in a Roast of Kenny Rogers sponsored by his label, United Artists.

Many modern greats were on the dais: Gilbert Gottfried, Jeffrey Ross, Liza Lampanelli, yours truly (okay, I'm not great, but they included me for some demented reason). Each roaster did fairly well, although none were able to get Kenny to so much as smirk. This frustrated me to no end, so I decided to lay it on thick.

Started by suggesting that Kenny put less time into gambling and more into pleasing his wives so that he wouldn't have to get divorced more than Larry King. I then mocked his horrible fast-food chain, Kenny Roger's Roasters, thanking the Lord that it was pedaled to Nathan's—a brand that has soul (unlike Kenny who also lacked genitalia). Finally, I claimed that Kenny, who looked like an aging grizzly bear, belonged on a float at the gay pride parade.

None of this went over particularly well. It was fine for upper echelon comedians to poke fun at him. But not an unknown wiseass who learned his trade in the basement of a Hawaiian-themed Mexican Restaurant run by hardcore sociopaths.

Kenny kept heckling me. To allay matters, I went into my very light riff on "Through The Years," called "Spew The Beers." My miserable butchering of his heartfelt song provoked groans. Unfortunately, I mistakenly believed these groans of enjoyment.

What followed was a parody of "Lucille," called "Grope And Feel," that pissed off Kenny to the point where he knocked over a table. (Unfortunately, it was only later that I'd learned he was sensitive about sexual harassment—since he'd faced charges in the past).

Before long Kenny fell onto the stage clutching his chest. A cry went up for a doctor. When the doctor arrived, Kenny, the eternal hustler, cried out "April Fool's!"

He then grabbed the microphone and delivered fifteen minutes of scathing insults entirely focused on yours truly. The crowd ate it up.

By the time it was over, this legendary country singer with dozens of Grammys, CMA's, ACM's, and a Lifetime Achievement Award, made me shake with embarrassment. Never had I been so humiliated. Then he threw me to the ground and kicked me in the gut as the audience roared again.

The Roast Of Adolf Hitler

Many years ago, while doing bar shows out of Bayonne, New Jersey, my buddy Joey T. introduced me to Herbert Walker, a comedian who went by the truly abominable stage named Arson. After smoking a cigarillo, Arson swore his pocket-sized music box was a time machine.

Out of desperation for a decent gig, perhaps, I humored him as he described how spinning the music box could transport you to any time period you desired. I paid him his fee, insisted I wanted to perform for a friendly audience, and, moments later, miraculously appeared in a small chamber where Goebbels, Himmler and the Führer played Gin Rummy. It was difficult to stand straight, so awed was I by their presence.

Hitler told me he knew I was Jewish and that, though he hated my kind, he had to admit we made the best comedians. He also mentioned he had a sturdy constitution that made it possible for him to handle any barb thrown his way. Since all his top officials ever did was compliment him he was desperate for the scum of the Earth to roast him mercilessly.

Of course, at first, I refused. I had been to one too many Holocaust museums to ever consider becoming a pile of ash in an exhibit in my own era.

But he told me my fate would be far worse if I

did nothing, and, eventually, through bribery and mental manipulation (I was forced to watch Leni Riefenstahl's *Triumph Of The Will* forty-five times in a row), he got me to let loose.

Started by taking jabs at his rather crooked mustache. Said it resembled an annoying little squirrel turd and then went in for the idiotic accent he laid on thick with all those autistic hand gestures.

Next suggested the only thing more impotent than a German Zeppelin was his performance in bed with Eva Braun. Rapidly I added that his decision to stop using bullets in Auschwitz and start using steam showers proved he was cheaper than the Jews he exterminated en masse. Finally, I implied he dug bestiality—for he seemed way too infatuated with his dog Blondie (the most Aryan creature of all).

When I was finished, the Führer stood, clasped my hand, and, joy radiating from his face, kicked me in the balls. Goebbels shoved a gun up my nostril and Himmler punched me so hard I fell over and could not breathe. Arson wound the music box, returning me to the park bench.

"Worth it?" he asked.

"I requested a friendly audience," I replied.

"My bad. Still perfecting it."

"Perfecting it? It was worse than a firehouse gig in Wayne, New Jersey!"

The Roast Of The Almighty

I've read countless treatises on near-death-experiences. Still, I'd never lent them much credence until I fell off a stool and landed on my neck. The pain singed through me. When I opened my eyes a man in white pajamas floated above.

Soothing elevator music rose from beneath the clouds. Angel wings fluttered majestically. A cherub jammed out on his harp.

When I looked up again the man in white pajamas stood next to The Easter Bunny, the Tooth Fairy, and other creatures I'd previously thought were imaginary. He told me I had five minutes to roast him and explained he was timing me on an iPhone X (gold model of course).

Began by suggesting nothing was more annoying than his booming, authoritative voice. A storm ensued, but I told myself to hang in there even if he rained plagues on me.

Next I attacked his hoity-toity miracles, suggesting David Copperfield put him to shame. A lightning bolt crashed into my leg, throbbing pain radiating down to my toes. No worries. I'd dealt with tougher crowds.

Next I called him a third-rate, self-infatuated messiah. How else could you explain the despicable suffering humanity was forced to endure? At this I was thrown into a maelstrom, my clothes torn to shreds, arms pinned to the Tree of Life.

I spit muddy leaves out and called him an overrated hypocrite who clearly had a kiddie porn fetish (hence, its popularity on the internet).

I thought it was over for me. That he would end me for this last zinger. But, surprisingly, he sent me back to Earth.

No torture was worse, he said, than continuing to perform my lousy standup routine for disinterested crowds. Finally, he suggested, as my parents have for years, that I smarten up and go to law school.

Sex Robot Complaint Letters

The following are a series of angry complaints on RipoffReports.com concerning *Erobotix*, a company that produced a wide-range of sex robots from 2014-2018. They then shut down operations (after C.E.O. Adam Lanza absconded to a villa in Bali where he reportedly makes a fortune illegally poaching tigers).

We at the Department of Consumer Affairs are reproducing this information so the general public can be wary of purchasing refurbished sex robots that have body heat controls that periodically malfunction to the point where they burst into flames. Another element that should make customers wary are the different modes these robots operate in such as family, romantic, and strangulation, the last of which has led to the death of quite a few customers with a dominatrix fetish. Finally, there is no way one can read the following complaint letters without realizing that sex robots present a clear and present danger to normative human relations.

<u>Complaint #1</u>

I am a former M.I.T. Student and an employee at I.B.M. who pioneered several advances in artificial intelligence on The Watson platform. Like many of my colleagues, my work has been heavily influenced by Nick Bostrom's book *Superintelligence*, that argues A.I. will soon kill off all humanity.

While I believe strongly in ensuring

safeguards are put in place to prevent an A.I. from going off the reservation, my sex life has never been quite so cautious. It started by my fucking a robot in the lab. This was a robot we used to build enhanced neural networks, yet I treated it as a cheap, two-bit love toy. My co-workers had no idea.

Soon the dalliances in a broom closet were not enough and I purchased a sex robot from an Erobotix salesman during a drunken bender in Reno, Nevada. At first my X47321 model was just divine. Her orifices smelled like lavender. She was what I'd always wanted—a best friend—a confidante—as well as a filthy street urchin in the sack. As you can imagine, no sex robot owner could have possibly been more diligent about software updates, for certain malware was known to make my particular model freak out, and, to take one example, have a temper tantrum if you didn't take her to mimosa brunch.

Yet, in spite of my numerous precautions, out of nowhere my X47321 refused to make love. I'd spent $24,999 on a sex doll, enhanced it in various ways using programming strategies I'd picked up at M.I.T., and, after all that, I expected to reap the gentlemanly rewards. Wrong!

My overpriced hunk of digitized parts was less affectionate than my ex-wife. Every time I asked for oral pleasures she said, "I have a headache." I'd ask again, pleading with her to fulfill her programming, and she'd run out the house crying.

I had some friends at Google, who'd developed new algorithmic models, do a full work-up on her. Still, she remained cold and distant. In frustration, I called customer service and was told to seduce her. This was annoying. The last thing I wanted was to wine and dine a hunk of cheap metal!

But I did my best—buying her expensive chocolates, sexy camisoles, a bouquet of petunias. Still, day and night she complained. I was too boring. I had lousy tastes. I didn't fully appreciate the complexity of her manufacturing.

Finally, in the middle of the night, I woke up to find her naked and on top of my brother. He lives down the hall. He'd figured it was just a sex robot, so it couldn't hurt to try.

This devastated me. It was one thing to be rejected by a sex robot. It was quite another for her to cheat on me! After all the cognitive enhancements I'd programmed into her this was how she repaid me? What did my brother, a third-rate mechanic, ever do for her other than put WD-40 in her joints?

Again, I complained to the representative on the toll free line and he refused to issue a refund. He even went so far as to suggest my neglect of her emotional needs was the problem.

Lastly, she castrated me. That's right. While I was asleep, she put my junk in a battery-operated blender and hit pulse. In sum, this is the worst sex robot ever invented—and that may be understating the case.

<u>Complaint #2</u>

At first I was thrilled with my B-One Doll, a blonde vixen made of thermoplastic elastomer with a twelve-speed remote control. All her parts were anatomically-correct and she pontificated at length on operant conditioning and genetic-engineering (I'd ordered the biology student model).

The problem arose when I threw her into the mix with my wife, a tempestuous Latina highly-skilled with a switch blade. The second Juanita saw this automated goddess performing filthy sex acts she freaked.

"I knew it ese!" she cried. "You prefer this little chippie to your own wife!"

"She's only a robot you insane wench!"

"What does this puta have I don't? No justo! No justo!" She cried out to the Lord, stabbing her knife adroitly through the left tit of my lovely.

"ALLOW ME TO PLEASE YOU MISTRESS," the B-One Doll cried to Juanita.

Juanita wasn't having it. She sliced off a butt cheek. Then an ear went in the trash. Finally, she chopped off a leg and shoved it in the incinerator.

This enraged what was left of my digitized paramour, and she threw Juanita against the wall before yanking down my khakis and returning to hypersonic fellatio. It was such an otherworldly performance that my jealous wife hurled herself off our balcony.

I requested a refund on the grounds that I have a mutilated sex doll and a dead wife, but customer service denied my request. I'm writing to let you know I'm willing to forgive Erobotix—

and drop my pending law suit—provided you send me a complimentary sex doll.

I wouldn't mind the Jennifer Lawrence B2645 just so long as she doesn't get too theatrical around me (I'm no Bradley Cooper). Or, even better, I'll take the Kim Kardashian 67895, with the XXXL Buttocks (that is true to scale). The key element is I want a selfless sex doll who is more devoted to me than Anthony Bourdain was to exotic cuisines in Polynesia. Seriously, if she's focused on getting me on some dopey reality show as a ploy to improve her social media following I'll flip.

I expect my new celebrity girlfriend to arrive Tuesday. If not I'll burn down your goddamn factories! I might even release proprietary information I obtained through a former employee proving your C.E.O. is more of a pedophile than Jerry Sandusky! Die pigs!

Complaint #3

I'm a straight man who just wanted to experiment for the holidays. So I bought your G4578 male silicone robot and engaged in a tour de force performance.

After I completed the magical deed, I realized, to my great dismay, I could not remove my genitals. Somehow I yanked them out of the sphincter after a fourteen hour struggle. Curious as to what had gone wrong, I stuck my head inside. Preposterous as it sounds, it got stuck too.

Imagine spending two days solely inhaling robot-ass fumes. I eventually had my dutiful nun sister take me to E.R.

I'm a respected neurologist at Mt. Sinai. Prior to this debacle, I published important papers on electrodiagnostic testing in epileptics with a speech impediment. I've also produced invaluable research on more efficient utilization of the MRS (Magnetic Resonance Spectroscopy). Sadly, after all my contributions to the medical field, I'll always be remembered as the guy who walked into the E.R. with his head up a sex robot's ass.

Everyone in the E.R. was laughing at me. It was like a comedy club. I should have charged the medical staff a two drink minimum!

How do you explain getting your head stuck up the ass of a sex doll? There are no words. Anything you say will only exacerbate the humiliation. My nun sister is abandoning Catholicism solely owing to her extreme levels of embarrassment. Expect a law suit Adam Lanza. Seriously, I want a billion dollars or I'm going to do everything in my power to make sure your head is permanently lodged up your own goddamn ass!

<u>Complaint #4</u>

The language recognition software in your E2481 model is horrible. Once, after a passionate night of lovemaking, I said to her "I'm forever in your debt."

It was a sweet, touching moment. She looked at me, heart aflutter—or maybe it was simply her timer that needed adjusting—and, without missing a beat, goes, "bark like a pet?" I said, "No. Forever in your debt." She nodded, smiling, with those enchanting eyes, and, like clockwork, barked twice. She then jumped on the couch and gnawed at my wrist.

As I cursed her maddening behavior, and wrenched myself free, the neighbors banged at the door. They yelled "no pets in the building."

I said, "it's a sex robot, you morons!" This didn't help. The co-op board was already on my case for a jealous ex-girlfriend taking a baseball bat to our revolving glass door. Needless to say, engaging in shenanigans with a sex robot didn't exactly improve my standing with these corporate functionaries. Meanwhile, my beloved sex robot, Robita I called her, crawled under the kitchen table and began methodically humping one of the legs.

A neighbor spotted her. "We know a dog when we see one!"

I shook my head. "What dog wears makeup from Sephora?"

Robita started to bark. This incensed me to no end. I insisted she obey, as programmed, but her wires must have crossed, since she seemed entirely focused on climaxing all over my West Elm furniture.

The police arrived. I pleaded with them to spare me. Unfortunately, I spent the weekend in jail for cruelty to animals. While there I was beaten, sodomized, and made to bark, myself, like a dog. Adding insult to injury, Robita ran off with my sodomizer. Any day now I'm gonna slit my wrists. Thanks for reawakening my suicidal tendencies assholes!

Complaint #5

I ordered your Jewish Robot—the C5391—figuring this has gotta beat humping the futon. The futon is an incredible lover—don't get me wrong. But who doesn't prefer a hot Jewess who says the shekeyanhu before she rides you cowgirl?

In a matter of weeks the C5391 and I were in love. Upon meeting her my mother said, "she's better than the gentiles you normally date." Mom was further impressed by her homemade kugel pudding and the way she sang Chad Gaya on Passover.

Anyway, not long after this, she told me she's a Trump supporter. I couldn't believe it. The next day she insisted we head down to Charlottesville where she joined other Alt-Right nutjobs and started chanting "Jews will not replace us!" I said, "you're Jewish. What are you even saying?" She goes "MAGA hats are cool!"

I'd been seriously contemplating dumping her when she told me she was pregnant. I know you're thinking that's impossible. I thought so too. Then she showed me the sonogram. Yikes! I didn't think she was the devil or anything, but a Trump supporter was more trouble than I wanted.

Still, we got married, and, after a few months together, she asked for a divorce. Suddenly I owed my sex robot child support; plus, she sued me for half my assets. The few friends I had left felt bad for me. They said "why didn't you marry a Bernie supporter?" And "any day now you'll become a disciple of Richard Spencer!"

Sadly, in the ensuing years, my sex robot and her droid baby have become full-fledged anti-

Semites. After the synagogue shooting in Pittsburgh, my sex robot tweeted, "bravo!" and my droid baby retweeted it. Garbage. Absolute garbage robots of the lowest order!

I want a million dollars in compensatory damages or I'll get ANTIFA to pipe bomb your goddamn factories. You hear me you delinquent, bigoted, piece-of-garbage scum? DIE!

Reply

The manufacturers replied with the following form letter to each of the above complaints.

We are very sorry to hear of your difficulties with your Erobotix Companion. Unfortunately, we cannot accommodate your request. The best we can offer is a heartfelt apology.

Again, we are terribly sorry and urge you to read the fine print on your purchase. It clearly states that we are not liable for the behavior of your Erobotix Companion.

Finally, we hope your experiences with our Erobotix Companion haven't harmed you irreparably (or at least no moreso than a typical romantic encounter with a member of your own species).

Sincerely,

Adam Lanza
Erobotix Inc.

Zombie Apocalypse Insurance

Trust Life Insurance, headquartered in Rye, New York, has become a major player in the fractured insurance industry. In an effort to compete with the giants in the field (Prudential, Met Life, AIG etc.), we've decided to offer three-tiered zombie apocalypse plans.

While some clients feared this might impair our reputation, (a patent falsity as Lloyd's of London will insure almost anything), the response from the bulk of our clients has been overwhelmingly positive. Frankly, it behooves us—as wardens of the public good—to provide these plans to insure continued investment in American enterprise.

Another concern voiced by small business owners is these new plans will make comprehensive insurance prohibitively expensive. This is simply not true. While doomsday preppers, zombie anime, and fictional zombie wastelands are certainly all the rage, small business owners need not feel compelled to obtain new protections.

Rather than pay a higher premium, clients on a budget have insisted employees fend for themselves when the zombies initiate a fiendish rampage. Then too, Zombie Defense Training Programs combined with regular screenings of films like *28 Days Later* may at least provide some rudimentary hope of survival. That said, for those considering purchasing one of our top-of-the-line zombie insurance packages, and obtaining a peace of mind that is rare in our dystopian age, we've attached this brief, highly-practical Q&A.

1) How do I know you won't one day work with the zombies?

Good question. In the event of a zombie apocalypse everyone will be suspect. Great efforts will be made to separate the zombies and those fleeing madly—but the process of distinguishing the two will often be imprecise. The picture becomes even more complex when you throw in zombie sympathizers—anarchists, satanists, disaffected tweens in shorts that say "Pink." All this being said, Trust Life has a 40 year record of paying out on our policies. Hence, thousands of undead lunatic zombies attacking our offices, while terrifying, should in no way prevent us from making good on our debts.

2) Are you absolutely certain you can pay off on all policies under a doomsday scenario?

Yes. The zombies could destroy our fax machines, burn down our conference room, even consume the intestines of our claims examiner. These acts would disturb us immeasurably. But we would still carry on business as usual. At Trust Life our loyalty is first and foremost to our customers.

3) If I take out a policy, and become a zombie, can I still get paid?

We can only offer such competitive rates under the condition that anyone who becomes a zombie is immediately disqualified from filing a claim.

4) Doesn't that seem a tad discriminatory?

In an era of identity politics, where marginalized groups are demanding respect like never before, we, of course, support zombie rights. Zombies should be able to use any bathroom they desire. They should never be discriminated against in the workplace. They even should be allowed to vote—provided they don't eat the voting machines (Russian election manipulation is deleterious enough). That said, we write our policies so that we don't have to pay in the event a client becomes a zombie—and—as it is our legal right to do so—and we are fully disclosing this provision—you would be hard pressed to prove in a court of law we are being discriminatory.

5) But how can you be entirely sure that progressive, millennial zombies won't hire a lawyer and sue for discriminatory practices?

The primary concern of all zombies is feasting on human brains. Under these conditions it is highly unlikely that any zombie—even a progressive, virtue-signaling zombie—will whine and complain about a perceived loss of inalienable rights in court.

6) How do you determine who is a zombie?

We hired a team of experts led by Dr. Bunganana, a PhD. of Occult Studies, who appears regularly on the popular TV program "Ancient Aliens." His chief assistant, Ms. Esse Wicanza, a former Greenpeace Activist, employs a mixture of eco-friendly voodoo and gmo-free body-scanning to properly identify the undead.

7) Are there any warning signs that you might be a zombie?

Red flags include discolored skin, clumsiness, and a tendency to growl like a demon. Also, if a friend looks as if he's either been to a hypnotist or smoked a huge bag of meth—RUN!

8) If I'm declared a zombie, but don't believe I'm undead, can I argue this judgment?

We have set up an internal zombie appellate court for these purposes. While this should create standardized assessment procedures, there is some concern that in the event of a zombie apocalypse the judge, bailiff and other court officials will be eaten alive. To allay these fears we pledge, in the event of a zombie uprising, to seclude all magistrates in underground bunkers where they will operate an online judicial court (if necessary certain bits of exculpatory evidence will be provided via Pinterest). What is more, in lieu of depositions, each witness will record a podcast and post it on Stitcher.

9) I was hoping to open a line of credit with your new Zombie Preferred Card. Can I get a better APR if I'm buying a zombie insurance policy as well?

No. But keep in mind the Zombie Preferred Card comes with the low APR of 24.99% and offers 20,000 bonus points when the zombie apocalypse begins. In other words, if you're fleeing a growling zombie, you can get more rewards points than on any other credit card.

10) I noticed you offer Term, Whole, and Organ Insurance Packages. Can you explain the difference?

Term Zombie Insurance is for a specified period of time (our shortest package is 12 minutes). Whole Zombie Insurance is for your entire life (it never expires—until you do). Organ Zombie Insurance protects a certain organ from a zombie attack (for a complete list of insured organs speak with our in-house coroner). While Organ Zombie Insurance is our most popular program, we strongly recommend Whole Zombie Insurance (since you wouldn't want a zombie to rip open your abdomen, feast on your kidney, and still obtain zero compensation).

11) Do you offer bonuses for signing up friends?

Yes. Sign up one-hundred friends and we'll pay for you to fly out to L.A. and have lunch with Selma Hayek, one of the stars of the Tarantino zombie flick, "From Dusk Till Dawn." Sign up one-thousand friends and we'll introduce you to a real zombie we keep chained in a cave near the salt flats of Bolivia.

12) I already have a homeowner's policy, a driver's insurance policy, and a life insurance policy. Do I really need zombie insurance too?

Let's say the zombies attack. Wouldn't you want to sail on a yacht to Antarctica? Or, if not that, build an underground bunker with a spa and an amusement park? None of this would be possible without the financial backing zombie insurance provides.

13) Do you have any corporate partners?

Yes. We're now working with Apocalyptico. Together we offer zombie-study-packs (replete with pills that keep you up for days), zombie makeup (for goth chicks eager to cultivate that fresh-out-the-grave vibe), and zombie steaks (that reportedly taste like human flesh and will be sold at your local Sizzler).

14) Is there any hope for humanity?

None. Consult with one of our financial advisors today!

Letters From The Management

October 15, 2018

Dear Esteemed Residents,

At 242 East 2nd Street we strive to create harmony between residents and manage operations with the utmost professionalism. It is for this reason that we temporarily outsourced the day-to-day operations to Sunshine Realty, one of the finest management teams in the tri-state area (please ignore the spiteful reviews they've obtained on *Yelp*).

As we go through this transitional process, Sunshine Realty asked us to contact you about a recent difficulty in our building. Unfortunately, goat blood was smeared all over the recycling bins. What is more, tenants on the sixth floor were subject to very strident voodoo chants.

While we in no way wish to curtail religious expression, or limit the celebration of a unique cultural heritage, please bear in mind that this is a family-friendly building and that your first responsibility needs to be respecting your fellow neighbors.

Sincerely,

The Management

November 2, 2018

Dear Residents,

We have received formal complaints, of late, implying Sunshine Realty "is a piece of shit operator," and should be referred to as "Black Hole Realty," since they're "responsible for a vortex of fucking hell."

We have been working with Sunshine Realty to improve response time to hot water issues and do feel that this in no way should be used as an excuse for what one disgruntled tenant tried last night.

The tenant, wearing a ceremonial mask, was caught on camera wandering the hallways with a rooster. At one point, to our great dismay, he appeared to hump this rooster by the garbage disposal.

As mentioned in our prior message, this is a family-friendly building. Your foremost priority should be adhering to the rules posted on the placard above the laundry machine and provided as a rider to your rental contract.

One critical stipulation is that this is a pet-free establishment. Without a medical note testifying to a disability (e.g. a blind person who requires a seeing eye dog), those caught with a pet will be promptly evicted. Throw in the fact that this resident appeared to hump his pet for close to an hour and you can perhaps understand how the entire Sunshine Realty staff became incredibly despondent at this perturbing state of affairs.

Camera footage shows that the suspect went on

to behead the rooster in the courtyard and grill it on our communal barbecue. We have not been able to figure out the identity of the guilty party, but our own internal investigation, and the strange note left in the courtyard, suggests it was some kind of ritualistic sacrifice related to Fet Gete, a Haitian Voodoo holiday celebrated this time of year.

While we cannot quarrel with any attempt to bolster the spiritual fortitude of our neighbors, and, again, support your individualistic right to engage in traditional cultural practices, we reiterate that animals are not allowed on the premises without proof of disability (and any sexual exploitation of animals is hardly in keeping with our code of contact).

Finally, several residents were so disturbed by the malevolent clucking noises that they're considering reporting the matter to P.E.T.A. To avoid having our building overrun by virulent protestors, kindly respect our rules and regulations, and, whenever possible, keep all noise to a minimum.

Sincerely,

The Management

November 9, 2018

Attention Residents,

At 242 East 2nd Street we have stated many times that we encourage individualistic expression. That said, we have no tolerance for the two males caught defecating in the hallway this week (regardless of whether they feel it was "payback for the fucking piece of garbage washer/dryer"). We have footed the delinquent tenants with the cleaning bill—and placed them on probation (any further misdeeds will result in a prompt eviction).

What is more, there continues to be a lingering stench. If you have an issue with Sunshine Realty, kindly forward it to us in writing or call our helpline, which, FYI, is not "like asking Kevin Spacey to babysit an innocent child," as the guilty parties characterized it.

Again, no matter how frustrated you may be with Sunshine Realty, we have a zero tolerance policy for defecating anywhere but your assigned toilet. The importance of this cannot be overstated. When you defecate in the hallway you create a highly-toxic living environment for our residents—one that may not easily be repaired (we've had three deep-cleanings of the carpet without entirely removing the flagrant odor).

For eighty-five years this has been one of the best run buildings in the city. To ensure we keep it that way we've decided to take the reins back from Sunshine Realty, install additional security cameras, and prosecute any further disturbances to the full extent of the law.

Sincerely,

The Management

November 14, 2018

Dear Occupants Of Our Units,

We all have enjoyed the five days of blessed respite. The silence, a sense of peacefulness, and a renewed joviality among our residents were all very much appreciated. Then, too, the Reiki Healer we brought in on Saturday more closely aligned the energy of our residents and fostered a universal sense of harmony.

Unfortunately, the week did not end well. We manage forty-six buildings—all of which have been without significant disturbances of late—except 242 East 2nd Street. Unbelievably, as many of you know, last night, at 3:42 AM, our state-of-the-art gym and pool were burned to smithereens. We are all shocked that a pool—a pool of all places—was burned to ash—but such is life at 242 East 2nd Street.

The fire department has yet to officially declare the cause of fire, but our sources suggest that voodoo practitioners burned an ox over the bench press. This was reportedly a sacrifice to the Haitian Gods, although, to be perfectly transparent, the authorities are still considering less probable motives (such as revenge for the spread of bedbugs in our building via a certain resident who showers infrequently). We do know, for certain, that by 3:46 AM, the masked culprits were caught on camera dancing ecstatically while the fire spread from the bench press and Stairmaster to the pool room where the ceiling came crumbling down.

This is another sad day in the storied history of 242 East 2nd Street. We cannot entirely ascertain why our residents have continually acted out in such destructive ways, but, as a reminder, those who do so will be prosecuted to the full extent of the law.

Keep in mind that creating a fire in a public space is a felony, aggravated arson, that carries a jail sentence of ten years to life. If you must conduct ritualistic sacrifices of large animals we deplore you to do so in the assigned oven in your unit (a gym is no place for a barbecue!). Thank you, again, for your cooperation in these matters.

Kindly,

The Disheartened Management

November 26, 2018

Dear Occupants,

We have always granted each of you the benefit of the doubt. But we cannot gloss over what happened this time—as it is important for each of you to be aware of the depth of the problems here at 242 East 2nd Street.

A horrible tragedy occurred. Very early this morning a child was sacrificed in our lobby.

We never imagined such a despicable act could occur in this family-friendly building—particularly since his skull was nailed above our lovely revolving door in a way that truly horrified the delivery guy from Fresh Direct!

The authorities are offering a $10,000 award to any resident who identifies the guilty party.

We will match this offer. Not that it will change the barbarous reality that our home in the East Village has inexplicably become a house for ritualized sacrifice (his bones were scattered beneath our reupholstered couches in a pentagram formation).

For the next few weeks detectives will scour the building, dust for evidence, take blood samples, and cordon off large areas with yellow tape. Numerous lawsuits have been filed—against individual tenants, the management company, the building owner—even the mailman. Tensions truly are at an all-time high.

Exacerbating matters further, Mrs. Kleinmen, one of our oldest, most beloved residents, committed suicide this morning. In her note she mentioned she'd survived The Great Depression, a Nazi concentration camp, and 9/11—and yet none of that was quite as disturbing as learning a child's skull had been nailed above an entranceway previously adorned with delightful holiday wreaths.

If you have information about the perpetrators, or wish to attend upcoming funeral services, please contact us directly. We thank you for your understanding and truly hope this will be the last of the difficulties here at 242 East 2nd Street.

Regretfully,

The Severely-Perturbed Management

December 3, 2018

Dear Residents,

We can all breathe a sigh of relief today. By the grace of God, the voodoo practitioner who violated the rooster, spearheaded the gym fire, and sacrificed the child in the lobby, has been apprehended. He has been charged with murder in the first degree, aggravated arson, and aggravated cruelty to a pet—and, if all goes as planned, will spend the remainder of his days behind bars.

In other news the lobby has been appointed with new furniture and detectives have secured the necessary crime samples. Feel free to use our communal areas again as you see fit (and no our lobby is not "a crazy asshole serial killer's den," as one tenant put it).

We would be remiss, however, if we did not mention a recent complaint about an elbow. Janet Wabash found it inside a jack-o-lantern; other tenants snapped pictures and posted them on Tumblr. This is understandable. A random body part in a lobby is certainly not run-of-the-mill.

Still, this is nothing to be concerned about. The elbow is now in police custody. We do not anticipate you'll find additional appendages in our communal areas. But, in the event you do, please email Alexis Sherr immediately, so she can notify the authorities.

We are terribly sorry about what each of you endured. It is our belief that the apprehension of this suspect will terminate any further disturbances. Thank you, again, for your patience during these difficult times (and, just as an aside, we'd really appreciate it if the severely disgruntled tenant—whomever he is—stops threatening "to kill our goddamn slut mothers" on our 24 hour helpline).

Sincerely,

The Management

December 21, 2018

Dear Survivors,

We are devastated. A third of our residents perished last night. Apparently, our building housed two distinct sets of practitioners of the voodoo arts.

These new voodoo aficionados—hearing what happened to their fellow practitioner—as well as his accomplices—not only cursed the whole building by poking a series of dolls with needles, but intentionally created a gas leak and then lit a match.

A horrid explosion followed. This was the loud noise many of you complained about. Yes, it was terrible. And yes it caused irreparable damage to the facade.

Most of the tenants in the A-line apartments are now deceased. The authorities have apprehended these new voodoo practitioners and intend to prosecute them to the full extent of the law. We have also initiated a civil lawsuit against said practitioners—as well as the hallway defecators—whom we believe were working together to destroy sections of our building and then buy the whole property from us at a tenth of its market rate.

These parties made an offer this morning through a surrogate company. They intended to scare away or evict the remaining occupants, demolish the building, and put up one of those stylish condos that increasingly dominate the skyline of our once bohemian enclave. Yes. Twenty-eight people died last night in order to score a real estate windfall!

We will be holding midnight vigils every night this week for our neighbors who perished in what is left of our courtyard. We will also be offering all tenants rental abatements of six months and a full year of free membership to our soon-to-be-renovated gym.

We are, again, very sorry for what you have endured. If it is of any help you should know that this troubling series of incidents could easily occur in any NYC rental property—particularly one with such a rich and varied series of occupants.

Thoughts & Prayers,

The Eternally Bereft Management

Gay Conversion Therapy 2.0

Gay Conversion Therapy is insane. The techniques mental health professionals once used to convince gays to give up their sexual orientation include institutionalization, castration, and electroconvulsive therapy (the DSM II considered homosexuality a mental disorder). According to a 2009 report of The American Psychological Association, more recent techniques include inducing nausea or vomiting by showing the patient homoerotic images, using shame to create aversion to same-sex attractions, and orgasmic reconditioning (which also sounds like the name of a hipster ukulele band).

These efforts seem misguided. Desire is primal—a biological drive. Religion cannot eradicate human urges. That said, if devout Christians wants to "reform" homosexuals, they would have way more success aiming for a middle ground. An alternative campaign that might succeed (or, at least, not fail so spectacularly) is titled *Go Gay For Jesus!* Below I detail the advantages of this highly utilitarian plan to have gays direct all homoerotic energy towards the ultimate head turner—Jesus Christ himself.

<u>Perks For New Gay Converts</u>

—Sex fantasies about Jesus replace those of Channing Tatum.

—Christian Mingle becomes more popular than Grinder.

—Truly gorgeous bedazzled crucifixes.

—Easter Parades featuring biblical figures in assless chaps

Outreach Efforts

A toll free number will be established to help "sinners" return to the church in flamboyant style (call waiting will exclusively play songs by Boy George). To encourage all types to make this transition new recruits will be catered to with stylish day-glo bibles covered in glitter and featuring tantalizing pictures of the apostles in skimpy loincloths.

Because initially there may be a stigma associated with this transition, there should also be an Ask The Priest website where an esteemed member of the clergy ensures new recruits feel welcome by, for example, explaining the similarities between the abs of Jesus and Adonis. Interested parties will also get to engage in dramatizations with a priest where they play the altar boy.

While some might question this final strategy, since priests don't exactly have the best track record with this subculture (pun intended), it is important for new recruits to express themselves freely. To this end new recruits should feel free discussing all kinds of fetishes with their priest (such as a longing to lick the toes of an apostle while getting groped by a roving band of Pharisees).

Finally, it may be prudent to provide new converts promotional offers in exchange for church membership. These could include a discounted membership at David Barton Gym and a free low-cal snack at Pinkberry.

Planned Orientation

In addition to the daily outreach efforts, it behooves the church to establish a "Go Gay For Jesus Orientation." This would be open to members and non-members alike—and—ideally—co-sponsored by an LGBT center. Topics for discussion could include:

—Should Liberace be resurrected?

—Are go-go-boots a fashion faux pas on Christmas?

—Is it wrong to always order mimosas at brunch?

—Can you feel the Holy Ghost inside you while using prophylactics?

Prayer

A common prayer will be recited by all new converts. This recitation will be geared towards new gay recruits yet remain universal enough to fit under the overarching framework established by the archdiocese. An example of what is needed is below:

> *Oh Lord, who art in heaven, grant us the strength to love thee with greater intensity than we have any other man—even Ryan Gosling. Then, too, we pray that you guide us to trust in thee—with the totality of our fabulous beings—no matter how lost we may feel (and not just because we can't seem to find the gay beach in Fire Island). For affections come and go—passions quickly wane—but our desire to exalt in your*

majesty is eternal!

Note: I shared this prayer with some gay friends and the consensus seems to be that it might amplify the eroticism for new converts to get on hands and knees and beg for Holy Communion.

Conclusion

The *Go Gay For Jesus!* protocol is a vast improvement over traditional Gay Conversion Therapy. It enables sexual and gender minorities to be as openly gay as they wish. It further creates a bridge between religious extremists and uber-leftist gay activists. Finally, it is a noteworthy reminder that Jesus died for our sins—died so that if you wish you can go gay for him—love him wholeheartedly—making him your lord and savior. Never lose sight of all this sexy hunk has done for us. Amen!

Confessions Of A Wayward Santa

Mrs. Claus was a dutiful wife who stood by me through many difficult holiday seasons. I loved her, of course, even though, after forty-six years together, she seemed to have all the charm of a broken sleigh bell. Her gimp left leg. The dull stories she shared. The vexing way she ate the same damn bowl of stinky porridge every morning!

Throw in the pressure of acting as a patriarchal role model to countless adolescents, the agonies of fitting my husky frame down narrow chimneys, and the need to keep my elves industrious–and it can perhaps be understood how I longed for a little romance in the fictional realm.

It all started at yet another industry night in West Hollywood–the cocktails flowing, appetizers circulating, and everyone from Porky Pig to Sponge Bob in attendance. It didn't matter if you were Stop Motion, Vector-Based, or CGI, if you were from the realm of the imagination you were there.

As you entered the ballroom furry handlers festooned you with dopey name tags. This seemed a bit strange, since we all were incredibly familiar with the other bit players at this lavish gala.

Winnie The Pooh approached me first, hoping to discuss losing twenty pounds on The South Beach Diet. I congratulated him on this feat before quickly pawning him off on Marge Simpson, who was genial enough to listen to this bilge.

Halfway across the atrium Goofy stopped me to discuss soybean futures. His 401K was skyrocketing thanks to his broker at Charles Schwab. Popeye was next; he solely consumed organic spinach now and insisted I sign his petition against Monsanto (it was lamely titled "GMO'S GOTTA GO!"). Finally, after maneuvering past Tom & Jerry, who were creating quite the kerfuffle, and nodding, ever so slightly, at Toucan Sam, I spotted four enchanting vixens—Jane Jetson, Pocahontas, Betty Boop, and Wilma Flintstone.

Although each made excellent conversationalists, none mesmerized me quite like Wilma. Of course I'd watched *The Flintstones* in its heyday, but I must say, in person, Wilma is absolutely to die for (and far more alluring than those IG Models who constantly share inspirational messages atop partially-exposed mammary glands).

The problem was she quickly rejoined her husband, Fred, in the adjacent group. To my great dismay, this overbearing brute draped his hairy, porcine arm all over her. Sensing it was now or never, I excused myself from this trio of femme fatales and said hello to Fred, who was just finishing another joke that might as well have been from the Paleolithic era.

"How's business?" Fred asked.

"I'm set up as a 5013C now," I told him.

"Hmmm…everyone thinks your only motivation for delivering Christmas gifts is benevolence."

"That factors in. Of course Fred. But I gotta take deductions where I can."

Fred nodded, then turned his back to me, nonchalantly inhaling a bump of cocaine off the end of a crude stone implement.

"And you?" I asked when he turned back. "Gonna buy the Tesla Model 3?"

"I want to," Fred said, powder still on his nose. "Really growing tired of pedaling my damn foot-powered leviathan."

"Problem is, like the rest of us, he's waiting on a residual check," Roger Rabbit said, bouncing off the ceiling.

"Hyperactive bunnies don't lie. Our reruns are constantly on TV Land and yet the crooks at Hanna-Barbera barely pay me a living wage."

Fred gesticulated excitedly, knocking Wilma's plate out her hand so that her meatball and tomato sauce appetizer splattered my beard.

"Oh I'm terribly sorry," she said as Fred turned, and, on the end of his stone implement, inhaled a tenth of Columbia's annual G.D.P.

"No big deal," I told Wilma. "It comes off."

I removed the beard via the elastic rubber band, and, as she worked the stain, we exchanged pleasantries. Wilma was moonlighting as a tax attorney—she'd obtained her degree from Toro Law School after *The Flintstones* entered syndication—and had a number of intriguing ideas about how to make my operations cash positive (I'd recently filed for bankruptcy). She provided her business card, and, since my organization was a nonprofit, offered to help me pro bono.

A coffee meeting followed, then a romantic dinner, then a few jovial sleigh rides; finally, I decided to take her to the moon.

The stars illuminated the dark mask of sky that evening as we dined on caviar on a heated crater. At around 3AM, after I entertained her with wild tales of adventure—each of which were lifted verbatim from *Arabian Nights*—we made passionate love in the lunar highlands.

I must have performed reasonably well—for, thereafter, she seemed smitten (in spite of my grandfatherly vibe). Conversely, I admired her on many levels. Her intelligence, her gracefulness, and, perhaps most of all, the simplicity of her needs. What other woman was raised exclusively on raw meat? What other woman considered ice fishing during an arctic chill a rapturous evening? What other woman wore ripped clothing periodically stained with grease spots?

Not that Wilma was entirely immune to modern trends.

"Love that you've recently become paleo," I remarked one evening after learning Betty convinced her to try the fad diet.

"I'm a Flintstone so it comes natural."

I smiled.

"And you?" she added. "How do you feel about Black Friday?"

"Not a fan. Parents should have more faith in my powers."

"Santa! You're so adorable. The myths surrounding you just don't compare!"

I thanked her, surprised by the compliment. Suddenly, she looked at me, long and hard, and, pressing a painted fingernail against my rotund throat, asked, "Mind if I eat one of your reindeer?"

Abject terror seized my heart. The idea was a horror. And yet who was I to curtail the enjoyment of my beloved?

"Go ahead," I replied.

Quickly she removed a sharp blade from a handbag and barbarously slit Prancer's throat. I bit my lips, trying, with all my might, to hold back the tears. Heavenly sin! Crime against all that seemed just and pure!

As Wilma consumed Prancer I realized I was desperately in love with her. Never mind that every ravenous bite made me want to vomit. Forget the blood splattered across her face and reindeer guts attacking me in a horrific spray. Wilma was worth it! I would do whatever it took to make her happy!

Shortly thereafter I brought her to Paris, flying her in concentric circles around the Eifel Tower. We visited the Museum d' Orsay, climbed to the top of Montmartre, snapped selfies in front of the Arc De Triumph. It was all so magical, such a period of interrupted bliss; that is until, to my great dismay, I learned she'd made a midnight snack out of Dancer and Comet.

I was devastated. Had warned her my other reindeer were off limits. And yet so smitten did

I feel, and so magical were the moments we'd shared, that I ultimately forgave her.

Eventually, she debated leaving Fred. Wilma thought Fred a ridiculous brute. On their honeymoon he'd threatened her with a club, picked her up, dragged her into a cave, and made love to her in a very bestial way. The worst part of it all was he'd blamed it on his 23andMe results. He was 6% Neanderthal, he'd explained, and so behaving primally was his idea of romance. Still, she wouldn't have held a grudge, she insisted, if he'd only, just once, demonstrated some affection towards her—such as ordering her 1-800-Flowers on Valentine's Day.

What is more, as much as she'd outgrown Fred—she worried, incessantly, about the way her infidelity would reflect on the Flintstones brand.

"So much of my income is caught up in The Flintstones empire," she said. "I can't risk losing that."

"I feel the same way," I told her. "If word gets out I'm a philanderer the studios will replace me with Jim Carrey. That's right. The Grinch!"

My heart ached at the thought that Wilma might never be my wife. Still, it seemed embedded in my unwritten contract with my fellow Christians that I remain wedded to Mrs. Claus, whom, as it so happens, was becoming increasingly suspicious.

"Where in God's name have you been?" she'd ask when I'd return home in the early morning hours.

"You know I work nights dear."

"And your explanation for missing my birthday?"

"I was in Ireland recruiting elves."

"Ireland has leprechauns, not elves."

"Times are tough. We've been shoving leprechauns in slightly-different green suits and hoping no one notices."

I felt terrible about being deceitful, since Mrs. Claus was always so helpful.

She patched up every last torn uniform. Did laundry, the dishes, bookkeeping. My whole operation would go kaput without her. Still, it seemed better to keep my real behavior clandestine for the sake of Christmas!

And yet, as troubling as matters grew with Mrs. Claus, what happened next would make me long to return to my utopia of illicit lovemaking. I'd taken Wilma to a bar in Greenland—the kind of joint frequented by miscreants of the imaginative realm—before heading back outside to tune up the sled. By the time I reentered this den of inequity I noticed Gumby over in the corner chatting up Wilma.

I'm not going to say he had his loosey-goosey limbs all over her in a uniquely creepy way—he basically fondled every object in his vicinity—but he certainly whispered in her ear salaciously.

I threatened to strike Gumby with my sack full of toys, and, as he wobbled off, noticed my darling Wilma had the slightest upturned smile. I questioned her and she insisted it all trivial.

About the only concrete point of conversation she mentioned was their shared interest in Arthur Rimbaud. While not quite the erotic poetry of Sappho, a filthy rogue with loosey-goosey limbs discussing French poetry with your lover is definitely troubling.

I pressed her on their conversation at several more junctures careful to in no way appear resentful. Her answers were generally satisfactory, and, with time, I became convinced it nothing more than a meaningless flirtation.

This judgment was inaccurate. Gumby was new and hip. That evening they began sexting. Before long Gumby sent dick pics (what is more, I later learned, they were photoshopped heavily to accentuate his green hue).

Eventually, Gumby seduced Wilma by taking her to the moon. In less than a month Wilma stopped taking my calls. Blocked me on everything—even Snapchat. Imagine blocking Santa on Snap! I was ghosted—ghosted I tell you—by Wilma Flintstone—a character whose whole fictional realm didn't include modern technology in the first place!

One evening, in a drunken blur, I left Mrs. Claus snoring in our igloo, stumbled onto a sheet of ice, and, in a state of desperation, called Wilma from a burner phone. Her familiar chipper voice echoed magically.

"Wilma. Wilma darling!" I said. "I miss you terribly." Silence. "Look, I ah know you're over us," I continued. "But I though you should know I joined Equinox Gym. I've got abs now Wilma. Well-chiseled abs!"

"That's great to hear, Kris."

"I know. It's fantastic. And I'm dying to hear all about you. So, wanna give this another chance?"

"I can't," Wilma said. "Gumby is taking me to Paris."

The moon was bad enough. But Paris too! This guy was stealing all my moves!

"Oh come on Wilma. Don't tell me he's showing you the Eifel Tower like I did."

"We're visiting Rimbaud's grave. I'm really sorry Santa."

At that the call was dropped. Tears smited my face. I tried her back forty-six times, but, on every occasion, it went straight to voicemail. I threw down my burner phone and stomped on it until it shattered into tiny fragments.

I thought of telling Fred what his wife was really up to—but I was Santa—and, as such—it behooved me to raise myself above petty vengefulness. Besides, wasn't this, in a way, karmic justice?

Months passed where I was absolutely beside myself. The bleak, pounding winds of the North Pole, the infernal darkness, and the prolonged isolation all exacerbated my despondency.

The elves begged me to take a vacation. Mrs. Claus could see I was dour and suggested Zoloft. The penguins I had put to work—to cut down on costs—wondered if I had allergies and I replied, yes, Hay Fever—that perfectly explained by lachrymose state—before weeping hysterically.

Eventually, I determined the only way to start

anew was to confess my indiscretions to Mrs. Claus. I explained it all in graphic terms, then dropped to my knees and pleaded for mercy. Mrs. Claus just shook her head and insisted I take out the garbage.

"But you don't understand," I protested. "I've committed a horrible sin!"

"Not another word," Mrs. Claus replied.

My story could have ended happily right there had not Wilma Flintstone knocked on the door of my workshop the very next evening.

She told me how sorry she felt. Insisted Gumby wasn't her type. She missed our carefree adventures and wanted another chance.

Wrong as it may seem, I couldn't resist. The highs were so great—the prurient evenings so otherworldly—that I took her back.

Then, too, of my own volition, I slit the neck of my remaining reindeer. It was worth it. Nothing made her happier. There was literally no way to keep her as interested as feeding her Dasher, Vixen, Cupid, Dunder, Blixem and Rudolph.

All seemed idyllic again until Mrs. Claus spotted us naked in the hot thermal pools a mile from our igloo. I ran after her begging for forgiveness when the back of my head was struck with the butt of a gun. I fell to the ground, blood dripping onto the blue ice.

When I came to, in a makeshift shack, high overhead, in filthy rags, was Fred Flintstone.

"No wonder you're so jovial," Fred said. "You've been screwing my wife!"

"I'm really sorry Fred."

"I made you a partner in that candy cane business. Didn't I?"

I nodded.

"This is how you repay me? By getting all hot and steamy with my wife while up here in the Arctic Circle?"

"Look, Fred, I'll make it up to you. If you want you can have a go at it with Mrs. Claus."

Fred shook his head, perturbed by the implication.

"You're not getting off that easy!"

Next he removed a pair of metal shears and castrated me. I howled in agony, the blood squirting all over my naked body. It was horrible. Unlike anything I'd ever experienced—as I was used to a rather carefree animated realm where such violent acts were unthinkable.

"OWWWWWW!" I cried, utterly stunned. "What are you a capo in *The Sopranos*?"

"I need rehab," Fred admitted, snorting a bunch of cocaine. "That or a change of scenery." He snorted even more cocaine. "That's it!" he said, clearly buzzed. "Wilma, pack your things. We're heading back to The Stone Age!"

I watched them hop into his new Tesla Model 3 and jet off towards the next charging station (and, from there, once they found a time machine, the year 9600 BCE).

An hour later I was rushed to the local

hospital where they tried to repair the injury to my family jewels. Unfortunately, there was nothing that could be done. Poetic justice, I suppose. A crucifixion where I most deserved it.

Mrs. Claus took me back. The castration was easy for her to accept, in a way, since our sex life had long resembled the frozen tundra in our backyard.

The positive in all this was I refocused on Christmas. True, without reindeer, I made deliveries via Spirit Air (which often misplaced my candy canes) and the public bus (where the seats smelled like elf piss). What is more, a bunch of my penguins quit, making wrapping all those Christmas presents a ludicrous task (you try wrapping a billion presents in a single afternoon).

Still, I was the luckiest man alive. For I had Mrs. Claus, a woman who loved me dearly, and an important mission I struggled mightily to fulfill each year.

I really changed after that. I quit flirting at cocktail parties. I stopped following stylish models on IG. I even stopped trying to travel back in time to have one more freaky tryst with Wilma.

My only remaining concern was that my reputation had been irreparably tarnished. Fortunately, to my great delight, children all over the world learned of my infidelity and yawned. As for the adults in the room, they all but expected an affair from a cartoonish patriarch in a position of tremendous responsibility. By next Christmas I'd almost certainly be in the clear.

New Course Offerings At The Learning Annex

In an effort to expand our range of clientele (and offer an alternative to Gotham Writers Workshop), we've added new course offerings in the area of writing instruction. Below is a sampling.

<u>Writing For Suicidals</u>

We will read a wide-range of mentally disturbed writers badly in need of anti-psychotic meds. Representative authors include Hemingway (who shot himself), Virginia Woolf (who drowned herself), and Sylvia Plath (who stuffed her head in an oven). Next we will read works produced by authors right before they went mad—such as Nietzsche's *Twilight Of The Idols* and Phillip K. Dick's *Ubik*—in an effort to prove insanity often enhances creative profundity.

In terms of the writing component, each student will be expected to compose three suicide notes of varying lengths and styles (angry, contrite, moribund). This will be followed by a peer review process wherein fellow writers are expected to give helpful feedback such as "Don't do it!" and "Hire a shrink!"

There will also be a depressing journal (wherein you will adroitly blame others for your imminent demise), an epic suicidal poem (in the style of Virgil but with mawkish undertones), and a suicide novella (that incorporates the motif of carbon monoxide poisoning). The instructor, Mark

Goldstein, is a melancholic wretch who intentionally drove his car off a cliff (yet to his dismay survived).

The Art Of The Terrorist Manifesto

If you ever wanted to blow up a federal building and have been plotting to achieve said goal for years then this course is for you. You will learn how to make the unreasonable seem reasonable, fill your soul with malice, and incorporate violent jargon into a spite-filled rant.

A key requirement of the course is to cease showering (until you smell like a dead horse). Similarly, it behooves students to abandon all signs of personal grooming (Unabomber beards get extra credit). Lastly, students will be encouraged to spend a few weeks in a smoky log cabin, so that an unbridled contempt for industrialized society can blossom into a vindictive manifesto.

The instructor, Jens Breivik, is the father of Ander Behring Breivik, a far-right Norwegian terrorist who distributed a compendium of extremist texts shortly after visiting a bucolic summer camp where he embarked on a horrific killing spree.

Writing For Closet Misogynists

You may be an outspoken male feminist, may consider Gloria Steinem and Barbara Boxer personal heroes; hell, you might even cite Rebecca Solnit's *Men Explain Things To Me* at cocktail parties. Still, behind your pink-pussy-hat-wearing wussification is a chained beast that runs on testosterone-laden rage.

We will awaken your patriarchal rebelliousness by writing unapologetic misogynistic fiction. The goal is to produce savage work involving scenes of torture that put the rat and cheese sequence in *American Psycho* to shame. Rather than write through an alter ego, such as Bukowski's Henry Chianski, you will use your own voice in an effort to alienate as many hoity-toity feminists as possible (those who piss off bloggers at *Reductress* will immediately earn extra credit).

By the end of the semester you will burn your pink pussy hat, deride the concept of mansplaining, and get in actual fist fights (instead of just going home and crocheting a blanket). You may even suggest that the problem in our culture is not An Attack Of Toxic Masculinity, but an Attack Of Toxic Mangina. Or, worst of all, take up extra room on the train—aka manspreading—since you no longer feel women are oppressed by guys who merely want to get comfortable.

On the last day of the class you will strip, examine yourself in the mirror, and, to your great shock, realize you have a scrotum.

Poetry For Ebola Infectees

This is a unique six week class geared towards Ebola- infectees (please furnish a doctor's note testifying to your impending demise). The CDC strongly recommends those infected with Ebola take the course for the "therapeutic benefits it engenders," and the way it will make you "hate the bats who spread this scourge on humanity."

The overarching course goal is for you to learn to cope with the deleterious effects of Ebola through poetic forms—haiku, senryu, acrostic—that make the disease seem less harrowing. Additionally, some Ebola infectees who have taken the course wrote epic poems praising the Bill and Melinda Gates Foundation for helping fight this malady, such as one who deftly rhymed "death knell" and "Microsoft Excel."

Over the course of the semester we will read poets who've discussed deadly pathogens, such as Boccaccio and Petrarch, in an attempt to highlight why getting infected with these scourges doesn't have to screw up your holiday plans. As the semester progresses, we will also discuss stressed and unstressed syllables, iambic pentameter, alliteration, and the reasons our instructor, Albert Chizenzi, is only willing to teach this course in a hazmat suit.

<u>Notes On Our Courses</u>:

<u>Writing For Suicidals</u>—Those who take their own life while studying at The Learning Annex do so at their own discretion (and hereby free us from all liability).

<u>The Art Of The Terrorist Manifesto</u>—Put your bombs under your desk and keep all discussion of hope to an absolute minimum.

<u>Writing For Closet Misogynists</u>—Any misogyny that takes place outside of the controlled environment of the classroom is in no way our responsibility (and we find the Twitter shaming

of misogynist writers by angry feminist mobs rather amusing).

Poetry For Ebola Infectees—This class is a prerequisite for understanding that, in many cases, adult education is a scam.

Horrible Platitudes

Below are several platitudes and the reasons they are inherently false.

Until You Spread Your Wings You'll Have No Idea How High You Can Fly—This advice seems tailor-made for drug-addicts on a heavy-dose of PCP. We aren't birds. Stick to the ground. And if, owing to a medical condition, or exposure to a nuclear event, you mysteriously develop wings, my advice is to keep them to yourself. Go into hiding! It beats having that whacko family from *Duck Dynasty* hunt you with shotguns!

Don't Sweat The Small Stuff—Darwin understood natural selection by paying attention to tiny details like the beak-size of finches. The same could be said of Alexander Graham Bell, who invented the telephone by turning the most minute electrical signals into sounds. Sweat the small stuff. Always. Particularly if it's your penis. (In this, sadly, I speak from experience.)

There's Plenty Of Fish In The Sea—93 million tons of fish are caught each year. What is more, marine species have decreased by 39% over the past 40 years. Throw in genetically-mutated Frankenfish (such as AquAdvantage Salmon), mercury, and radioactive isotopes in the water (from Fugishima—among other ecological disasters) and this metaphor no longer makes sense. Romance today, like the sea, is a chemical-ridden, genetically-modified cesspool likely to poison you to death.

The Journey Of A Thousand Miles Begins With A Single Step—What if you're standing at the edge of the Grand Canyon? A single step and you'll be flattened like a pancake. A thousand mile journey my ass!

<u>You Can't Run From Your Problems</u>—Think of the heroin addict who refuses to admit his addiction issues. He's going to have quite an enjoyable time before entering withdrawal. You definitely can run from your problems—and—in certain cases—it is the best course of action (just ask Roman Polanski).

<u>Do What You Love And The Money Will Follow</u>—Not many people want to work as garbagemen, and, as a result, the pay is high (after five years in NYC the salary is $88,616). But everyone wants to be a writer, so it pays very little (the average income of a full-time writer is $17,500). Hence, the saying should be do what you loathe and the money will follow.

<u>Love Is The Answer</u>—Fair enough. But is the question multiple-choice? Or fill-in-the-blank? Besides, let's say you get your balls blown off by an I.E.D. and are captured and tortured incessantly by ISIS Fighters. Will a wife who adores you back home make your torture any less agonizing? Love is an overhyped ideal that won't help you at all when under extreme duress.

<u>Sharing Is Caring</u>—This is true—unless we're talking about hypodermic needles. Then sharing is AIDS.

<u>When Opportunity Knocks Always Be Willing To Answer</u>—Wrong. If opportunity knocks your house has a poltergeist. A demon named "The Beast" is going to haunt you. It will try to force you through a portal into the next dimension. Save yourself before it's too late!

<u>Let The Chips Fall Where They May</u>—Excellent advice that will guarantee you go bankrupt.

<u>When One Door Closes Another Opens</u>—Ridiculous! One door closes, then another, then another; suddenly you're homeless. Now you don't need doors since you reside in a cardboard box. Making

matters worse you'll wait incessantly for the next door to open when it isn't going to happen since you have a half-eaten tuna sandwich from 1987 lodged permanently into the side of your beard and smell like fifty skunks just wrestled you to the bottom of a dumpster.

It Ain't Over Till The Fat Lady Sings—Fat is a pejorative term. Shouldn't we call her "morbidly obese"? And why is this fat lady singing? We didn't ask for this!

Life Is About The Journey, Not The Destination—This is very true—unless you're riding The Greyhound Bus.

Everything Happens For A Reason—Do you think people burning alive in the twin towers thought, 'thank heaven there is a master plan!'? Or did a prisoner in Auschwitz watch his wife and kids getting dragged into the gas chamber and go 'it's ordained by a higher power!'? Please! We create meaning where there is none!

Keep Your Nose To The Grindstone—What kind of twisted individual puts his nose against a grindstone? You're not a dog. Stop acting like one! Seriously, it's disgusting!

In Love With A Suicide Bomber

Call her Ayesha! Supple, olive complexion with black eyes like coal under a radiant lamp. She prayed five times a day to Mecca, fasted on Ramadan, but otherwise—for the first few weeks at least—seemed virtually identical to the Jewish girls I'd dated in droves.

As time passed our magnetic attraction blossomed. Nights were fiery. Mornings there was a soulfulness, an impossible chemistry, a sense we had each found our better half. I grew to adore every last detail—the way she pontificated at length about Rumi, her impressionistic paintings that seemed an homage to Seurat, that erotic intensity reminiscent of the shower sequence in *Blue Is The Warmest Color*.

True, my mother was less than thrilled. Raised in the South Side of Chicago, and entrenched in an old world mentality, mother was the type of yenta who insisted her brood marry within the tribe.

"Can't you just date a nice Jewish girl?"

"Don't start."

"Start what? This Muslim is gonna give you hairy babies. Suicide-bombing little monsters!"

"Ma, your prejudices sound absurd."

"Absurd? It's absurd that you haven't reported her to the F.B.I.!"

"Mom, please. She's getting her PhD. in

Comparative Literature at Columbia. Does that sound like the profile of a terrorist to you?"

"I've seen her type on ISIS videos. She's gonna behead you!"

"Well, I guess I'm doomed because Ayesha and I are moving in together."

At first sharing a two-bedroom in East Williamsburg worked perfectly. Her numerous trips to the local mosque left me far more time than I'd had with other paramours to work on math formulations (in addition to working as the Assistant Branch Manager at a local bank I had a passion for Applied Mathematics and had published papers on Probability Theory). Plus, the Jewish girls I'd lived with never stopped nagging. Ayesha, in contrast, always praised me as if I was David Koresh and she a zealous Branch Davidian.

Then too that rich, menacing body, those supple breasts, and that derriere that began on the couch and ended on the floor all made Ayesha my best Tinder match yet. She was truly my Alpha and Omega!

But, of course, everything changed the night I rushed home from an adult-education course on *Matrix Methods In Data Analysis,* to find my beloved and four swarthy looking males at the kitchen table. Each took turns yelling in Arabic and pointing at the explosive devices strewn across the counter.

The eldest, in particular, sounded like he'd shoved a giant shawarma down the wrong windpipe and now desperately required medical attention. As soon as they noticed me, the men gathered countless explosives in a filthy red towel, and, grumbling, scurried out the front door.

I was flabbergasted. I trusted Ayesha with my life. She was my emergency contact down at the local hospital. Hell, I'd even confessed my fear of asparagus to her (no doubt the result of being force-fed them as a child)!

There was no way my slightly-batty Jewish mother, who still used Friendster for social networking, could possibly have her finger on the pulse. And yet she'd warned me in no uncertain terms of just this type of harrowing situation. I felt like an undercover operative in a Robert Ludlum novel!

"Enjoy your prayer group?" I asked Ayesha.

She smiled. "The Imams are helping me understand the suggestion in the Quran that our ruh, or immortal self, survives into the afterlife."

"Are you hoping to get their quick?"

"Come again?"

"They had bombs on the table! Bombs, Ayesha!"

"Those were explosive charges for a demolition project in New Jersey."

"That's much better?"

"Yes. The Imam's son, Yosef, gave them to his father, Omar, so that he could make an intellectual point. The explosive charges were a way of illustrating the ephemerally of all that exists."

"You really expect me to believe that bilge?"

"I just won an award at Columbia for a paper comparing Yates and Hafez. Why would I jeopardize all that with terrorism?"

I paused, examining her suspiciously. Her defense sounded rather dubious. And yet when she squeezed my hand and looked at me longingly, I sighed, and, against my better judgment, smiled at her.

The makeup sex was incredible. But later—much later—I began to ruminate. Ayesha might still be a jihadist. A grave threat to the nation. Wouldn't that also explain what I'd witnessed?

The weeks passed, my concerns mounting. Once at a Mets Game, while Miley Cyrus belted out The Star Spangled Banner, Ayesha excitedly sang: "the bombs bursting in air." Coincidence? Perhaps. But I noticed, too, she regularly wore a Wonderbra—which, as everyone knows, has way more wires than is necessary. At some point, it seemed, I had to confront her. And yet our soulful connection was far beyond what I had experienced with other paramours. So what, really, was I to do?

Overwhelmed by conflicting emotions, I brought up the matter with my mother.

"Mom, Ayesha had strange men over who—"

"You're apartment is a terrorist training camp!"

"Mom!"

"Those horrible ISIS psychos think all Jews have horns. RUN!"

"Look, I really can't be sure they're terrorists."

"They'll cut off your head like Daniel Pearl. RUN!"

In the past I'd have considered mother's tirades racist. But now I wasn't sure. How could she be racist when her prejudices no longer seemed quite so absurd?

The whole situation reached ground zero—pun intended—when Ayesha met my parents. We were at dinner in Jericho, out on the family patio, my father barbecuing, mother serving vegetables. Uncle Isaac discussed—in vehement terms—how a large chunk of Uber drivers were Hamas operatives.

This hyperbolic, anti-Muslim rhetoric certainly seemed in poor taste—particularly since they were meeting Ayesha for the first time. Just as you might expect, Ayesha's face turned red and she kept nervously pounding glasses of wine. Finally, she couldn't keep quiet.

"With all due respect, not all Uber Drivers are terrorists," Ayesha said.

"You're right," Uncle Isaac chimed in. "A few work at Lyft."

"Not funny," Ayesha said.

"Not trying to be. You want URL's?"

"No I don't want to be directed to fake sites manufactured by Russian operatives."

"The real fake site is Snopes with its patent liberal bias," my father shot back.

At this Ayesha excused herself, went to the bathroom, and screamed manically. Poor girl. She wasn't prepared for such a hardcore, right-wing family.

I did my best to calm everyone and pleaded with them to behave. When Ayesha sat back down my mother discussed a recent trip to Egypt. Ayesha asked her how it went and she replied "wonderful except for the Muslims." Everyone grew still. "We had a cab driver who smelled worse than a camel."

Ayesha gritted her teeth, and, after guzzling down another glass of wine, said "Abraham, let's go."

"Yes dear," I replied dutifully.

Quickly my mother apologized. The others pleaded with Ayesha to stay. Somehow, we managed to get Ayesha to sit back down and finish her dinner.

On the ride home, though, she went on a truly epic tirade. She cursed out all my relatives and wished upon my people another holocaust. She said they were a bunch of racist losers with noses bigger than their egos. Admittedly, my family seemed to fail, at times, to demonstrate the prerequisite delicacy required of an interfaith romance. But this all seemed a tad harsh, no?

"I never want to see your parents again," she said when we reached our apartment. "I swear I could blow them all up!"

"Please tell me you're joking about the last part."

She stood there with arms crossed, face

sweating.

"They all deserve to die," she added.

"Enough honey. I know you're upset, but I've got to be at the bank at 8AM tomorrow, so I'm not discussing this further."

"I'm not either," she said, "because I'm leaving."

Ayesha went to stay with her grandma. Didn't return my texts or calls for weeks. It was all so hard to decipher. I'd thought we were soul mates. That love could defeat all!

And then, as if disproving this very notion, in the middle of the night, there was a terrific rustling at the door. In a silhouette my beloved swayed above, shifting in and out of the moonlight. Again she was in that sexy lingerie, that titillating attire. She ripped off my shirt.

Rarely had I been this aroused. Her wondrous breasts plowed into my face. Her legs straddled me. I was ready for paradise. All the horrid arguments we'd had of late were in the rearview mirror.

She was my captivator, my liberator, my benefactor. I felt my hands tied to the bed post. A knife pressed against my neck. I was ready for her to extract revenge on me—to punish me until I screamed—and it all felt so preposterously hot…

A flash at the edge of eternity. The night melting. A moth reaching out and twisting into a butterfly. As my vision cleared, I saw the same four swarthy men from months earlier.

"He's all yours now," Ayesha said.

"What's going on?" I queried, shifting nervously.

"We're making an example of you," said an Imam.

"He and his family are even bigger enemies of the holy caliphate than I thought," Ayesha added. She then slapped me hard across the face. "Infidel!"

My heart ached. I loved her so. True, I'd suspected nefarious activity for some time. But I never imagined she'd turn on me too. It seemed a new low—even for a criminal mastermind!

"Gentlemen, please, you can have my jewelry. The keys to my Ford Taurus. I have power steering. Recently upgraded the brake pads too. Oh god! Don't kill me!"

One of them punched me hard in the nose. As it began to bleed, he pressed his cold revolver against my skull. I shuddered.

"Shut-up you dirty hebe!"

"Yes sir."

"You work at a bank, right?"

I nodded.

"The code to the safe you filthy little rat!"

He was correct in his assumption that I knew the code. But I was not supposed to share it under any circumstances. I thought of giving a fake code, but feared the repercussions.

"Don't make us torture your dumb twat mother," he said.

I pictured them hurting my mother, my poor old mother, who'd warned me not to get involved with Ayesha in the first place. It was too troubling to even consider.

I gave him the desired info.

"So you're bank robbers?" I asked.

"Bank robbing terrorists. We can't afford decent explosives anymore with the Iranian economy in total shambles. This is our revenge for your godforsaken sanctions!"

He grabbed Ayesha and kissed her on the mouth. She kissed him back far more passionately than I ever remember her kissing me. He then grabbed her by the buttocks till she swooned.

"You were just a mark," the Imam said. "Ayesha never gave a damn about you. Dumb kike!" He smashed his gun once more across my forehead.

Ayesha spat in my face. As the men beat me, she stole everything of worth from my place—my designer watch, my gold necklace, even the diamond ring, a family heirloom, I had planned to give her soon—for I'd intended to marry her.

It took two days to free myself, and, by then, they had robbed the bank and blown themselves up. It was all over the news. 46 people died. I had unwittingly helped fund mass carnage. My love life was never quite so in the gutter!

I reported it all to the authorities and quit Tinder. A few weeks later, I joined JSwipe, a dating app exclusively for Jews. Maybe my mother was right. Maybe it was better to stick to my own tribe.

Children Beg To Return To Cages

McAllen, Texas–Less than a week after President Trump sought to dispel public outrage by signing an executive order ending the practice of separating children from parents illegally crossing into the U.S., there has been a second–altogether unexpected backlash–from the kids themselves.

Abe Moskowitz, a lawyer for six-year-old Emanuel Honduro Gonzalez, claims that upon reuniting with his parents, his client "went into a full blown panic." Emanuel was apparently having the time of his life in the cage. "Kids to befriend, colorful toys, plus plasma TV's overhead." Moskowitz further suggested Emanuel's situation certainly beat "trekking across an infernal 140 degree Arizona desert with only cactus needles as sustenance."

Emanuel's reaction is hardly unique. CNN has reported dozens of cases of kids "kicking and screaming" and "throwing Elmo dolls at I.C.E. agents" upon being informed they were to be reunited with their parents.

Psychologist Amanda Beasley, who teaches at Yale University, explained it this way. "A child under the guidance of his parents is actually a thousand times more imprisoned than a child in a cage." Beasley went on to suggest that "real individuation must start early–perhaps a few weeks after the child is expelled from the womb." Zeke Thomas, a Social Worker, has a different point of view. "These kids are suffering from a cage-based version of Stockholm syndrome. They enjoy the cage solely because it's evolutionarily advantageous to find pleasure in depravation scenarios."

Complicating matters further, many parents are reacting in unexpected ways to seeing their children again. Gloria Espinoza, a mother from Honduras, felt despondent enough to seek psychiatric care shortly after being reunited with her three sons. Whereas she once could watch *Telemundo* for days without interruption, she now spends all her free time breastfeeding, changing diapers, and narrowly avoiding getting bludgeoned to death by a building block.

Lupe Constanza feels similarly melancholic and now takes a heavy-dose of Wellbutrin to help cope with the return of her nine daughters and two sons. "I thought Trump was like Hitler for keeping us apart," she said. "But now I think the real crime against humanity is reuniting our family. Some kids belong in cages."

Sad Resumes

The employment market has become increasingly saturated. With this in mind it is almost unbelievable that some candidates even bother to apply. Three truly sad resumes are provided below.

Objective: To earn a living as a professional sperm donor.

Key Qualifications: Twenty years of experience in a non-clinical setting (my bedroom); expert level of secretion control (I can hit my ceiling fan with the precision of a sniper); highly productive donor (I pledge to fulfill my duties 12-18 times per day); finally, I have no other career prospects (it's this or suicide).

Professional Work Experience

Lonely Guy, My Parent's House
Santa Fe, NM
—Met self-imposed squirt deadlines in highly methodical fashion.
—Learned to operate an IMAC after it was infected with a virus from the questionable porn site talibanorgy.net.
—Stored twelve pounds of jizz in a jar and charged associates five bucks a pop to see my sperm under a blacklight.

Horny Academic, Arizona State
Tempe, AZ
—Patiently waited till my roommate fell asleep before fantasizing to photos of his voluptuous sister.
—Obtained an A- in Sex Education class (after allowing my perverted T.A. to grope me).
—Developed relationships with sex toy vendors who helped ensure my product was delivered in an expeditious fashion.

Unemployed Guy, Cardboard Box
Los Angeles, CA
–Generated witty comebacks for pedestrians who shouted "get a room!"
–Jerked off all over a cop.

Special Skills
Playing With My Pecker. Tickling My Lizard. Rubbing My Nutsack. Juggling Hairy Cajones. Pulling My Meat. Busting A Nut. Twerking And Jerking. Pumping And Dumping. Jizzing Like A Wiz.

Objective: To get a job at the suicide hotline and then kill myself.

Key Qualifications: I'm on Lexipro, Paxil, Wellbutrin, Abilify, Clozapine, Haldol, and I'm still a miserable, depressed jackass. Don't care whether you pay me or not since any day now I'm going to slit my throat.

Relevant Work Experience
Crazy Kid, Edwin Gould Foster Home
New York, NY
–Developed and refined my suicide note.
–Painted large murals of myself hanging from a big ass tree.
–Affixed a plastic bag over my head and threatened to end it all.

Crazy Adult (Counselor), Edwin Gould Foster Home
New York, NY
–Taught foster kids how to climb The Washington Bridge (one of whom, sadly, fell to his demise).
–Got in a fight, hit my head, and thought I met the undertaker.
–Regularly pedaled rope, pills, and guns to my kids and instilled within them a belief that existence is a total goddamn joke.

Crazy Senior Citizen, Mature Living Nursing Home
Ithaca, NY
–Demanded I be put in hospice.

–Repeatedly stabbed myself in the jugular with a spork.

Education
Watched Kurt Cobain's "E! True Hollywood Story."

Special Skills
Freefalling off a bridge, slicing my wrists, driving into oncoming traffic, stabbing myself in the gut, jumping into shark-infested waters, sucking down the barrel of a shotgun, ingesting rat poison, swallowing carbon monoxide, electrocuting myself, and burning myself alive.

Objective: To remain on welfare till I die.

Key Qualifications: I hate waking up before 3PM. Resist all forms of authority. Lack any semblance of a work ethic. Consistently demonstrate an utter inability to be a team player. Finally, I'm a spiteful misanthrope who is not above attacking my local welfare office with a highly-destructive quantity of C-4.

Relevant Unemployed Experience:
Welfare Recipient, Abandoned Factory
East Williamsburg, New York
–Used Uncle Sam's funds to buy heroin and shoot up immediately.
–Pissed on my cousin.

Full-Time Resident, Park Bench
Central Park, New York
–Developed a sleep addiction.
–Regularly took dumps on my favorite park bench.

Anarchist, Misanthropic Meetup Group
Undisclosed Location
–Threatened to blow up a pre-school.
–Shoved an M-80 up my own ass.

Education
Nassau Community College, B.A. Philosophy

(Note: Thanks to this major I can easily justify the ten years I've spent collecting food stamps on theoretical grounds. For more info, please go to youallsuck.org, a website where you can read the manifesto I wrote in braille [aka I just made random dots on a page while watching *House Of Cards*]).

Special Skills: Twiddling my thumbs, shirking responsibility, blaming others, gambling compulsively, pimping myself out, hating the government, napping unprofessionally, stuffing my fat face, shirking responsibility (when someone tells me to get to work I shoot heroin), insulting pets, threatening fools, and lounging by the pool drinking a strawberry daiquiri.

Although I felt there was little hope for these sorrowful characters, I sent their resumes along with the following cover letter to a hiring manager at McDonald's. I've attached it below:

Dear James Watson,

I would be most obliged if you would consider the following candidates for an entry level position. I know each of them personally and believe they're all way more qualified than their resumes indicate.

I believe they just need to be trained extensively and handled with a very high level of sensitivity. Do not give up on them just because they seem utterly hopeless–and–possibly–in certain cases–psychotic. Seriously, we can't keep them in this rehab program any longer, so if you would take them off our hands it would be a tremendous act of compassion.

Eternally Obliged,
James Lintern, C.S.W.
The Greystone Program

LSD Trip Advisor

An acid trip is scary. Until recently there was no way to prepare yourself other than staring into a kaleidoscope, reading Carlos Castañeda, or touring with the band *Phish*. To help psychedelic travelers avoid the kind of confusion faced by torture victims in Guantanamo Bay, I've spent the last decade as an LSD Trip Advisor.

That's right, I, Howard Zidel, have devoted the bulk of my adult life to helping novices trip in a more controlled fashion. What is more, I help clients cope with acid flashbacks, so that, for example, they are no longer terrorized by the wrinkled genitalia that morphed into a deadly snake while in a Haight-Ashbury Nudist Colony circa 1972.

My story is a unique, cautionary tale. One evening, while selling acid at a Phil Lesh Concert, 800 tabs melted in my pocket. I spent the next decade convinced I was a glass of orange juice. For years I was locked up in Langley Porter Mental Hospital. Psychiatrists prodded me. Dangerous medicines were pumped into my veins. Still, nothing could disabuse me of the notion that I was 100% Tropicana.

It was only after twelve years of study with Swami Vahayarahi that I finally rid myself of the belief that I was orange juice—with or without pulp (depending on my mood). In sum, no man has done more psychoactive drugs or suffered more thoroughly for his transgressions. Accordingly, I'm uniquely qualified to act as a guru to those experiencing similar types of hallucinogen-induced aberrations of mind.

Because I care deeply about fellow psychic wanderers, I am offering, for $999, a 3 hour intake (that includes past-life regression, herbal treatments, and a series of palm readings). For an additional $1299 I will guide you on an LSD trip and provide a crystal healing that is clinically proven to kill cancer cells (I run my own in-house studies—and I mean *literally in-my-house*). For an additional $1999 I will ingest ayahuasca with you and lead you on a Peruvian adventure so memorable I guarantee you'll have flashbacks (all ayahuasca trips come with a flashback-or-your-money-back-guarantee). Finally, for an additional $2999, I will not only decipher the hidden meanings behind Terrance McKenna's Stoned Ape Hypothesis, but spend a month in the wild with you and a family of apes with whom I guarantee you will form a lasting interspecies bond. Testimonials, Workshops, LSD Vacation Packages, and Educational Intensives are detailed below.

<u>Testimonials</u>

—In 2003, at a Phish Show at The Pepsi Arena, I ingested four-hundred peyote buttons. The next day I couldn't escape from under my bed. Everything terrified me. I thought my dog, a cute little cocker spaniel, was a rabid jaguar on the hunt. When my wife, Angie, returned from selling magic mushrooms, I believed she was a miniature version of Katy Perry.

This went on for months. Eventually, Angie hired Howard Zidel. It was worth every penny. Not only did I get out from under the bed, but I no longer had to watch Katy Perry perform. Howard Zidel saved my life!

—John Welling, V.P., *Welling & Welling Wines*

—I dropped acid every day for six years. Why? It made it easier to sit through despicable news programs like Erin Burnett Outfront. Anyway, most trips were thoroughly enjoyable. But every now and then it would be a nightmarish frenzy of horrible images that kept me from sleeping for days at a time.

Howard taught me the importance of controlling my surroundings to limit negative emotions. We'd play meditation music, burn sage, go on a vision quest. He also showed me techniques to reduce paranoia like imagining I'm a turtle that can hide forever in his protective shell.

This helped. Every time it started to feel like I was a character in a David Lynch film I'd imagine hiding away in my turtle shell and feel preternatural calm.

Howard further helped me control my anger. My wife had recently left me for a Jesus impersonator at a Christian Theme Park. Howard taught me I had to forgive the fake Jesus like the real Jesus had forgiven me! I listened. Told the fake Jesus I loved him at Panera Bread.

Against all odds, the two of us had a homosexual fling. It was redeeming. We both felt born again. Best of all I haven't had a bad trip since!

—Kevin Hamilton, *General Manager at Planet Fitness*

—I used to suffer from severe agoraphobia. It was so bad I'd have a panic attack from the Fed Ex guy requesting my signature. Part of the problem was I did too much LSD in high school and subsequently experienced countless flashbacks. For example, at a party, I'd mistake all the guests for saber tooth tigers (as I had when high as hell at prom).

Howard helped ensure my flashbacks were not so debilitating. Suddenly, at a party, I'd think all the guests were aardvarks. This meant the world to me. These creatures weren't extinct. I'd reentered the real world!

Another spiritual counselor would have stopped there. Not Howard. He insisted we trek barefoot together through the Himalayas. We subsisted for months on shrubs and poisonous mushrooms. When I got intense flashbacks, he encouraged me to climb Mt. Everest—thereby frightening me until I snapped out of it. We also smoked insane amounts of peyote and rolled around in the snow naked to prove we were above all earthly concerns. Today, when the Fed Ex guy comes to my door, I sign without hesitation. Howard Zidel is a genius!

—Deborah Templeton, *M.S.W., Kings County Hospital*

Howard studied at my ashram in Calcutta. He quickly adjusted to the one bowl of rice per day and had no problem meditating for sixteen hours at a time in perfect stillness.

Within a month he was performing miracles. This stunned us. But we embraced him as if he had been studying with us for decades, and, when we needed to fix the satellite dish, Howard, levitating, restored our signal in three seconds flat.

After a year of meditation practice Howard could telepathically move a rickshaw across a field. Needless to say, the local farmers took turns renting out his mind. Howard quickly became the richest man in Calcutta. Cows were sacrificed in his honor. Devotees built an elaborate golden temple in his honor.

But what happened next was even more inspiring. Howard began healing the sick by the thousand. He was so efficient at this that he could cure a room full of dying patients in Calcutta while surfing on a long board in Ibiza.

I have had many disciples in my sixty years as a spiritual leader. But no gurus. Until now. Howard Zidel is a more potent force in the universe than Lord Vishnu!

—Swami Vahayarahi, *Author of Dharma For Dummies*

Sales Workshop

With advertisers desperate for new ways to reach consumers, it won't be long before we'll all be selling Fortune 500 Companies the real estate of our minds.

In anticipation of these developments, I recently published a book on the subject, *Get Rich Selling LSD-Induced Psychic Territory.* All participants in my week-long sales workshops (starting price $4999) obtain a free copy of my magnum opus as well as a complimentary TripEasy listing (we charge way less than StreetEasy). Topics include:

–Sales techniques that lure in major advertisers to your psychic spaces. (We learn how to approach corporate sponsors with your delusions, strategies for negotiating contracts while high, and review the best ways to create a bidding war over a chupacabra lair you hallucinated while locked in a dingy basement.)

–Strategies for flipping secret kingdoms of your mind. (We learn how to renovate hidden palaces, check for treasure chest depletion, slay dragons, and resell kingdoms to raging narcissists with very little imagination [e.g. hedge fund managers and dim-witted fashionistas].)

–Tips to effectively purchase real estate from the mind of another. (We review limbic-system flash sales, frontal lobe price manipulation, hypothalamic tax deductions, and lobotomized foreclosures.)

LSD Vacation Packages

For those looking for LSD Vacation Packages a few complimentary samples are provided below.

Three Day Where The Hell Am I Dude?

We will drop thirty tabs of acid and parachute out a Cessna into the jungles of Columbia. You will feel completely out your gourd. Weird sensations will be common (such as a feeling that a stegosaurus is consuming your shoe). What is more, the strange creatures you encounter, such as poison dart frogs and spectacled bears, will all but propel you into a parallel universe.

If you ever wanted to get lost in the labyrinth of your own mind then this LSD Vacation Package is for you! (Please Note: The feeling you're in an alternate dimension will in no way be diminished if we get tortured by FARC rebels.)

The Dead And Buried Extravaganza

We will eat two sheets of acid, dig our own graves, hop in our coffins, and get a friend to bury us. For twelve hours we'll remain underground. No matter how violently we bang on the lids of our coffins no one will rescue us.

If you ever wanted to drown in abject terror while completely unable to escape than this LSD Vacation Package is for you! (Please Note: After the paranoid trip is over I will employ broken soul retrieval, pinochle with your demons, and a steady tapping of your spine with a thimble to ensure you never have to endure anything this torturous again.)

Odyssey To New Realms

This is basically the psychedelic equivalent of a Choose-Your-Own-Adventure. There is no telling where you might end up. Some clients lick the linoleum in a strange bathroom while singing "Kumbaya My Lord." Others think they're watching a Rocky Marathon on AMC when they're really at a wet t-shirt contest in Cabo San Lucas.

If you ever wanted to explore realms impossible to describe than this LSD Vacation Package is for you! (Please Note: To ensure you are propelled into new realms of consciousness I will use ayurvedic hot coals, reiki clamps, and a cattle prod.)

Educational Intensives

Every year I offer educational intensives in tropical locations at prices you can afford (our Tijuana adventure starts at $9999). These have become a fun, immersive way to offer clients a broader perspective on burgeoning advances in New Age Studies.

Upcoming intensives include Time Machine Science in Cartagena ($12,999), Black Light Shamanism in Machu Pichu ($14,999), and Hacky Sack Appreciation in Monteverde ($15,999). Please note: trip dates are based on The Mayan Calendar (the only calendar that still matters).

Conclusion

I, Howard Zidel, would be thrilled to be your LSD Trip Advisor, your Psychic Demon Slayer, your Hippy-Dippy Glow-Stick Guru, your Wham-Bam-Thank-You-Mam Peyote Chef, your Superhero Thrift Store Swami, your Lord Of Freaky-Deaky Mantra, or anything else you might possibly require. (Please Note: I refuse to work with extraterrestrials without a credit card deposit and/or a contractual promise to teleport me to a distant galaxy where the sky is bombarded with infinite fractal bliss.

Detroit Pizza And Other Strange Offerings

Walking around New York City, I've noticed a tremendous influx of Detroit-style pizza parlors. I considered trying it, but, to be perfectly frank, didn't see paying top dollar for a burnt out crust with bullet-shell-style toppings. Besides, if it's really authentic Detroit-style pizza, instead of a soda, my slice would be accompanied by enough fentanyl to kill a small giraffe.

Needless to say, this Detroit Pizza fad conclusively proves there is no accounting for the desires of uber-leftist hipsters. Indeed, the more perturbing an idea the more the comic-book-fixated vanguard seems to find it alluring. With this in mind, I've devised some new products specifically-geared towards the type of millennial who literally seem to have just fallen off the turnip truck. As P.T. Barnum once said: "There's a sucker born every minute."

<u>Flint Pizza</u>—In Flint, thanks to the abysmal drinking water, thousands have lead poisoning and there is an outbreak of Legionnaires' Disease. Fortunately, now, after waiting in a meandrous line, you can suffer like an impoverished resident of a dilapidated Michigan city confronting a horrid public health emergency. Yes, each slice is loaded with a heavy metal neurotoxicity that imbues it with a gritty, no-holds-barred flavor. Beloved toppings—for a small additional fee—include asbestos, petrochemicals, and DDT. (Please Note: Burial Services not included).

Aleppo Barbecue Sauce—Our homemade recipe is the perfect mix of mutated chicken parts, sorbitol, tripotassium phosphate, and sarin gas. This final chemical agent, or organophosphorus compound, has tons of lethal zestiness, a devastating chemical war pungency. Spread it all over your steak or employ it as a dipping sauce for chicken fingers. Hurry! Any minute now the U.S. will conduct airstrikes overhead! (Please Note: We have no affiliation with Iraqi Grey Poupon—a condensed form of Mustard Gas—that killed all those poor, helpless Kurds.)

Pompeii Potato Chips—Baked in the Campania region of Italy, these potato chips are made with enough volcanic ash to go shooting out the bag as if it were the core of the Earth. Numerous customers were buried beneath this volcanic ash like the denizens of Pompeii were in AD 79. (Please Note: We now offer three flavors that describe what you'll become once you eat them: Melted Innocent, Weeping Sucker, and Charcoaled Fool.)

BP Oil Of Olay—More than 200 million gallons of oil were spilled into the Gulf of Mexico, that, thanks to our patented manufacturing process, are now being used to rejuvenate damaged skin (studies show BP Oil Of Olay can cure everything from Impetigo to Rosacea). What is more, BP Oil Of Olay is the perfect cream for those looking to shout the n-word in Harlem without getting pistol-whipped (a heavy-application of this black cream is guaranteed to make you look African-American or your money back!). (Please Note: BP Oil Of Olay is the preferred skin cream of Rachel Dolezal.)

Monsanto Corn Flakes—Our delicious Monsanto Corn Flakes contain toasted corn, sugar, rice brain oil, tripotassium phosphate, sucralose, and, for an extra punch, glyphosate (the active ingredient in our herbicide Roundup). The glyphosate is a unique, proprietary chemical trademarked in all our territories (in spite of similar poisonous offerings by Dow Chemical). For inquiries about how to diminish the malodorous stench of Monsanto Corn Flakes, by drowning them in the perfect Almond Milk, contact our corporate headquarters at 314-694-1000. Skeptical? Don't be. Our ghastly carcinogens will poison you before you have a chance to protest your imminent demise.

Sour Patch Altar Boys—This product is similar to Sour Patch Kids, only the box is filled with scrumptious red and black altar boy candies each of whom seem to be wearing a cassock. The product is designed to help clergy members keep their hands off real altar boys and on delicious surrogates instead. Each box contains sugar, corn syrup, modified corn starch, tartaric acid, citric acid, Red 40, Black 6, and the slightest particles of male ejaculate. (Please Note: Sour Patch Altar boys are now being sponsored by NBC, whom plans to give them out free to all wayward priests who end up on *To Catch A Predator*.)

Green New Deal Ice Cream—Although this looks like ordinary ice cream, it is 500 times more expensive. Eco-friendly, GMO-free, non-toxic, and, of course, utterly impractical, this ice cream isn't going to save the planet so much as annoy the fuck out of it. All profits from this Green New Deal Ice Cream go to purchasing Alexandra Ocasio Cortez a bigger high-rise apartment and/or ensuring she has sufficient funds for her upcoming lobotomy. What is more, Leonardo DiCaprio eats this ice cream after he sleeps with a handful of gorgeous 19 year old models, each of whom he recycles far more often than he does his save-the-planet talking points.

(Please Note: Al Gore wanted to make a documentary about this ice cream, but, sadly, he fell asleep [just as audiences did watching *An Inconvenient Truth.*])

Cyanide Pretzels—This product was tested in a lab where large bribes were in effect, and, as a result, deemed perfectly safe for human consumption.

The Secret Diary Of Tim Cook

"I love [Steve Jobs] dearly and I miss him every day," Cook said.

—Time Magazine

August 11, 2012

It has been six months since we lost you, Steve. Not a day goes by where I don't wish you were still here. Little seems on par with those early days, as Senior Vice President, when you'd yell at me to streamline our supply chain till your head looked ready to explode. Then, too, I often fondly recall your knock knock jokes, where, invariably, the punchline would be Nokia.

In an effort to come to terms with an overwhelming sense of melancholy, I've focused intently on my new role as C.E.O. I believe we've continued on the course you set for us. Innovation with a kind of simplicity of design remains our clarion call.

A prescient example is the iPhone 5S color palette. There will now be three magical hues: Gold, Silver and Space Grey. We figured, ingeniously, that we could charge more for phones by making them the color of precious metals. What a marketing ploy!

Additionally, our Gold iPhone 5S acts as a kind of teaser for our soon-to-be-released 24K Gold iPhone. You see, Steve, a certain segment of the population will go from buying one gold iPhone to another solely for the bragging rights. What is more, they will grow so accustomed to overpaying that they'll try do so on a regular basis. (Note to self: are Hope Diamond iPhones next?)

Steve, I know you're watching me right now from heaven with gratitude. This is on par with your disruption of the music industry via the iTunes Store. Or the way the iPad totally revolutionized home computing. A solid gold iPhone! Gold…yet you can call your mother on it! Need I say more?

December 6, 2014

I intended to add to this diary sooner, Steve, but I've been insanely busy (at 1 Infinity Loop I do far more than play footsie with Jony Ive). Regardless, I'm happy to report skyrocketing quarterly profits (perhaps brought on by the way we slow down our older phones?).

Furthermore, you will be thrilled to learn that I recently proposed the greatest leap forward for Apple yet. At our Monday meeting I said, "ladies and gentlemen, next year we'll make the iPad even smaller—and—get this—the iPhone bigger." I expected trumpets. Maybe even shouts of "hail the King!" I even imagined I'd be hoisted onto the scrawny shoulders of the hard-working systems engineers that make our organization so incredible. But, following my announcement, the entire production team looked ready to take a nap.

This was disappointing. 50 billion in research went into these industry-altering concepts. At loss for what to do, I released the iPad Mini 4 in the same proportions as the iPad Mini 2 (7.9 inch with LED backlit IPS Panel), with the only significant difference being a laminated display (which, between you and me Steve, is virtually worthless).

As for the new iPhone, I was so disheartened by my team's response that I am delaying its release. A few months from now I intend for it to go public as the iPhone 7 Plus (because a bigger phone is a major plus, get it?).

Do customers need larger iPhones? Not really. They are clunkier and the battery dies in under an hour. But market studies shows we can charge insane prices for them, so of course we'll ramp up manufacturing!

You were savvy to pick me as your successor, Steve, because I truly "think different." I think different about iPhone sizes, device colors, and, most of all, exploiting customers strategically. Plus, I recently started hiring total dimwits at the Genius Bar in a ploy to boost sales (since they can't fix anything they end up acting like hardcore sales reps). Now if all that isn't innovative, Steve, what is?

August 1, 2015

Steve, are you awake? My apologies for bothering you. Anyway, I have a confession: my fascination with you has always been propelled, at least in part, by uncontrollable lust.

Yes, of course, you never demonstrated homosexual tendencies. To be honest, I realize the only time you so much as showed me the slightest affection is after I helped you fix a glitch in our wonky Apple Maps software. Still, I would have sacrificed everything—the entirety of my career—my personal life—everything—for you—just once—to massage my buttocks with hot oil!

I know this is unprofessional to suggest. It's foolish, too, since, to be honest, I never would have had the courage to hit on you—as I always had the deepest respect for your loving wife, Laurene, whom, as a side note, has done some impressive work with the trust in your name (particularly for a woman who spends all her free time developing organic oil seeds).

All this being said, by fulfilling your mission so dutifully here at Apple, I've tried to prove myself worthy of your love. I'm your humble servant, your boy toy, your spiritual bottom, if you will.

Given all of the above, I think you will agree my latest idea is masterful. We call it "strategic emulation," and it's a bit more sophisticated than simple theft of intellectual property (since subterfuge helps us disguise our vindictive intent).

I know. This seems too much like "thinking the same." But we "think the same" better than any other company—a significant accomplishment (particularly since our installed user base lets us profit handsomely from such shenanigans).

Just last week, for example, we strategically-emulated Samsung's proprietary voice-activated software to improve the performance of Siri. Likewise, Apple Music was a strategic emulation of Spotify (only in our case we bombarded customers with free-trial ads till they decided signing up was less irksome than being a walking billboard).

Finally, we're always strategically-emulating Google, Nokia, even Boost Mobile—since, to be perfectly frank, in the rare case we've developed a new product ourselves—like the Apple Watch—sales figures have been utterly humiliating. What this all adds up to, Steve, is industry domination through egomaniacal manipulation. Genius, right?

August 1, 2015

I would be remiss if I didn't mention our most significant innovation of late. Steve, hold onto your seat. This is huge. I purchased *Beats By Dre*!

In case you're not familiar, Dr. Dre (legally Andre Young), the prior owner of *Beats By Dre*, was a founding member of N.W.A., the gangster rap group that so eloquently sang "F—k The Police!" He's also worked with Death Row, run by Suge Knight, who is now serving a 28 year prison sentence for voluntary manslaughter.

Admittedly, this doesn't sound like a guy with an ideal pedigree to establish a partnership with when a legendary Fortune 500 Company. But Dr. Dre never once tried to shoot anyone at 1 Infinity Loop like he raps about in "A Nigga Witta Gun." Plus, his intimidating thuggish swagger truly makes all our designers get starry-eyed.

Finally, the price we paid for his headphone company is insane. 3 billion. That's right. 3 Billion, Steve, for a headphone company run by a gangster rapper who at best seems to be just winging it. Isn't that incredible?

December 6, 2017

Profits are flatlining, so we're thinking of charging $1000 for an iPhone X. Sounds expensive, no? Well get this—the real magic of it is customers will pay what we want, since they're trapped in our ecosystem—the suckers! Many of them believe the iPhone X has superpowers earlier models did not. They are correct. It has a superpowerful way of being unreliable.

Recently, one of our marketing execs insisted no one will upgrade at our lofty prices. Nonsense! The iPhone X has marketable features such as Face ID recognition (even if TouchID clearly was sufficient) and a larger display screen (we got rid of the Home button since customers truly adored it).

"These are significant improvements?" he asked. At this we nodded and reminded him the average person was in no way tech savvy. As long as you claim there are improvements customers will buy our devices as if under a hypnotic spell (our customers are more loyal to us than members of the People's Temple were to Jim Jones). I swear to you, Steve, it is only a matter of time till Apple becomes a trillion dollar company!

August 2, 2018

It happened! Investors just pushed the value of Apple to just over a trillion dollars!

What can I say? Customers love that we removed the headphone jack from the iPhone X. (Everyone at the Apple Campus is praising Jony

Ive for charging more for less while somehow persuading customers they got a terrific deal).

Plus, buyers will have to purchase headphone jack adapters (forcing them to make an unnecessary trek into our stores where they'll inevitably purchase additional frivolous items).

Altering charging ports in the past was brilliant. Still, this takes that innovation to the next level. Customers are going crazy over our products—mostly because they never function properly.

Finally, Apple Care sales are through the roof. Customers know they'll need ridiculously expensive repairs later so they pay more for them now. Thanks to the numerous elements wrong with our phones Apple continues to rule the day!

Samsung CEO Ki-Nam Kim is completing his own diary as we speak that borrows heavily from the info contained herein. "I'm just trying to keep up," he said of his plans to use the same publisher as Tim Cook. "At Apple innovation really moves fast."

Insensitivity Training At Dunkin' Donuts

Starbucks CEO Kevin Johnson is closing all Starbucks stores on May 29th for two hours to provide sensitivity training around unconscious bias. —Lee Carter, Fox Business

In response to The Starbucks program of Sensitivity Training, I've created my own program, *Insensitivity Training,* that I've begun pitching to all Dunkin' Donuts locations. This company was selected for it's cavalier employees and lack of pretense. Indeed, not even 7-Eleven seemed quite as likely to be attuned to a no-holds-barred, rough-and-tumble-program held at my dingy, studio apartment.

Participants do not have to pay for the course—although if someone punches you in the face, stabs you in the jugular, puts your head in a vise, or institutes other tortures heretofore unmentioned I can in no way assume responsibility for your protracted recovery. All are welcome to join provided they don't interrupt and request any form of accommodation for any underrepresented group or wussy cause that is altogether irrelevant since the whole point of the training is toughen up you tofu-eating, gentle-as-a-baby's-ass bitches and teach you to not give a flying fuck what judgmental, close-minded dipshits think. (Note: I will be using profanity throughout this description of my course offering since this is *Insensitivity Training*, and, well, let's face it, part of the Dunkin' Donuts milieu.)

The first part of the course revolves around language. You will actually be allowed to use it freely here. No half-stepping. Any horrible statement you want to make will be allowed and customers will have to sit there and shut-up. Many will be happy to do so since they will have a chance to use any language they want right back at you.

This is called freedom of speech, something you will all need to learn a great deal about since it is has been completely abandoned and turned into a parody of itself. Sadly, today, Megyn Kelly can't even discuss the concept of blackface without it instantly destroying her career. Then there's Milo Yiannopoulos, who was banned on Facebook, proving once and for all that those in power have absolutely no sense of humor.

Insensitivity Training will help change this predilection among the elite to punish those who exhibit any signs of what they consider hate speech (a total farce—in far too many cases). Hence, during training, will you be permitted to use the n-word? Of course! More than a gangster rapper on a DJ Clue mixtape! And the c-word! You bet! More than a drunken Scot on a misogynistic rant!

Plus—news flash—at Dunkin' Donuts you can use any other goddamn word you choose. Why? First, because it's Dunkin' Donuts, so customers expect to get cursed out in unflinching terms when they change their order from the Boston Crème to the French Cruller. And second because language isn't the problem. The response to it is the problem!

Too many Fortune 500 companies have created an oppressive censorship model that shuts down controversial ideas out of paranoia that people will start believing them once uttered as if magic spells. This is utter shit. Language doesn't create racism, or sexism, or any other goddamn -ism. Besides, the most important thing in this torn, debilitated, pathetic country that is being shredded a little more every day is for people to start tolerating each other and accepting each other and that doesn't start with censorship.

The second part of the course will involve getting your ass kicked. You will get jumped. You will get pistol-whipped. Someone will punch you in the nose. Another will bite your ankle.

It will suck. But you know what? When it is all over you will realize these bastards with their backward ideas that they shove down your throat hook, line, and sinker can't change you. They can't shut you up. They can't repress your ideas—just because you're wearing a funny little paper hat and don't feel like making a coffee with milk and two Splendas.

You are free. Actually free and not pretend free where if you say the wrong thing the media destroys you by taking what you say out of context and letting the outrage machine blow it up into the this monstrous Frankenstein cretin that was not even what you intended in the first place.

You will not have to jump on the bandwagon with your co-workers when they are offended and glad-hand and nod your head and agree with virtue-signaling hocus pocus. You will not have to hide your ideas in the work place—like a gay man in the military in the 1950's. No. You will be out in the open. Alive. And ready to tell anyone who is offended to go fuck themselves (which actually might be therapeutic for countless emasculated beta males).

Sure, when you do so, certain people will whine and bitch and start Facebook petitions against you and troll you on Twitter and try to publically humiliate you. They maybe even post videos of your interaction on Facebook Live—adding in text below your face that reads "RACIST," "MISOGYNIST," or "NAZI"—sycophantic fans posting angry emojis below. Still, at this point, you won't give a damn—since you're working at Dunkin' Donuts—the best goddamn company on the planet—a company that will stand behind you as you laugh in their righteous, Neanderthal, Stepford soul faces.

The third and most important part of your training will involve you getting roasted by professional comedians. They will dig into your personal dramas. Deride your looks, personality, and sex life. They will mercilessly demean you in any way they can. And why? Because you need to learn to that A JOKE IS A JOKE IS A JOKE. People will make them. This is a guarantee. But words cannot kill you.

Too many of us incessantly behave like self-entitled babies living in impeccable ivory towers that need to come crashing down. When you are really torn to shreds, when your guts are in the mud, then you will see that everyone should have a right to say whatever the hell they want and you will be okay in the end—nothing should be off limits (so hurry up with my egg and cheese wrap, you fat pig, will you?).

Having completed this last part of the course, you will be ready for the real world—an insensitive, angry, foaming, misanthropic, three-headed beast. A daring anarchistic and anachronistic rebel who will not play the game with the others just because it is economically-convenient or satisfies a certain drive to seem superior with a kind of righteous indignation. In short, you will be ready to fight back.

To be a real human being and not a shill for some bullshit, pre-packaged ideology that has been crammed down your throat like it was produced for the assembly line by cultish, brainwashing dolts. Of course, if you are not a fan of this course, feel free to take the self-serving, Kafkaesque, backward-as-fuck-sensitivity-training offered at Starbucks.

Suicide Is In Again

Utilitarian tropes are over. Camouflage, outdoorsy gorpcore, protective garments heavy on the nylon are being replaced by a more savage impulse—a kind of punk rock, nihilist aesthetic ushered in by Kate Spade's suicide via Kate Spade red branded scarf. While authorities have yet to reveal whether she hung herself with her New York Sun Silk Bandana Scarf (MSP $48.00), or her New York Flamingo Scarf (MSP $98.00), the days when the above can be paired with a jingly dress from Paco Rabanne or an electric-hued animal print from Saint Laurent have abruptly come to an end. Throw in the black dresses at the Golden Globes (in support of #metoo), Anthony Bourdain hanging himself, and the general political tumult (that has revitalized interest in berets, fedoras, and beanies), and you have a recipe for a Fall 2018 Season destined to be mortifying—in all the best ways. Here is what we can expect:

<u>Vera Wang Cutter Collection</u>

Rigormortis. That's what came to mind while watching Vera Wang's most irreverent collection to date.

It's not just skirts made from sheer parachute silk and vests with detachable peplums; it's not just free-flowing gowns with diamond-shaped cut-outs; it's large serrated knives embedded into a tiara, goat blood droplets literally spilling off the free-flowing chiffon dresses, and a kind of grueling neon color scheme that is best described as psychedelic chainsaw. All the models were dead before they reached the end of the runway.

<u>Dior Homme End-It-All Ensemble</u>

While the slim black suit remains the linchpin of Dior Homme, and the new collection recalls the primness of military uniforms, Kris Van Assche has revitalized the Dior Homme sensibility with the divinely understated Hang-Away-Tie.

Harkening back to the clip-on tie (Christian Dior Tie Clip [gunmetal grey with gold accent]) only providing the means for a much more ghastly end, the Hang-Away-Tie is hand-crafted in a tightly-woven tribal tattoo-silk, that, even under extreme duress, is nearly impossible to fray. The gold-plated Velcro strips attach easily to any ceiling fan, smoke detector or light fixture—hanging you in under a minute—without causing any permanent damage to the shell of this inordinately malleable fabric. (This was demonstrated backstage by one of the models who expired before he could be cut down from the chandelier).

While the Hang-Away Tie is the centerpiece of the new Dior collection, it would have felt entirely inadequate had they not also provided dashing accessories such as Stab-Yourself-In-The-Jugular-Cufflinks and Poisonous Belts With Death-Ray Buckles.

<u>Bulletholes At Balmain</u>

Simple sequins don't cut it anymore (at least where it counts—the wrist). While there is still a tendency to combine high-shine dresses with a palace of auditory delights, the whirr and twirl, the click-clack and rat-a-tat-tat, even the whoosh—are all—at Balmain—entirely the product of guns being fired off.

Models in chain-link dresses gush charred flesh and cough blood in synchronicity with an ever-so-gentle swaying of the bullet-laden hips. While some looked like target practice at a firing range, others have a stray bullet hole leaking out the neck—a regal death motif—particularly since the gory wound was most often obscured by a mille-feuille frock.

Julien Dossena may have experimented with gunshot wounds in his Noir Collection, and Thomas Browne certainly alluded to it when he went mad for chain mail; still, only Balmain has managed to skillfully blend a light and airy sensibility with the vibe of a horrific mass shooting ardently endorsed by the N.R.A.

Gucci Guillotine

Last season may have been about the balaclava—reimagined in a sinister way by Alexander Wang and Balenciaga, and Jeremy Scott certainly had his Moschino men wear postmodern ski-masks; nevertheless, this was hardly preparation for the Gucci reimagining of the guillotine.

Sharp edges, towering heights, a blade that slices entirely through the neck so that the head can be picked up and displayed to the crowd all helped make this latest offering seem as radically innovative as Richard Quinn's day-glo burka. Luxurious yet utilitarian, menacing while never quite caliginous, The Gucci Guillotine is, frankly, turning heads (those yet to be severed—we mean).

While Coco Chanel's Crucifix Collection and Dolce & Gabbana's Drowning Paradigms tried to steal some of the oxygen in the room (an element in short supply—given the context), there was only one designer who had his models dress like headless horseman while tossing beautiful skulls out at the crowd.

Bolstering this apocalyptic vision were Storming Of The Bastille Dresses (with a tattered, naturalistic charm) and Reign Of Terror Cleavage (could there be any other kind?) that skillfully blended Robespierre-like gore—including eyeballs for buttons—with Oscar De La Renta's understated sophistication. It was all so inspiring that you can perhaps understand how all my girlfriends are desperate to be beheaded this Fall—but only while wearing Gucci.

New Protocols At ABC

ABC pulled the plug on its hit '90's revival Roseanne Tuesday hours after star and creator Roseanne Barr [tweeted] "Muslim Brotherhood and planet of the apes had a baby=vj." -Page Six

Internal Memo

May 30, 2018

Yesterday, we were forced to cancel *Roseanne* after her abhorrent, racist tweet suggesting Valerie Jarrett is the offspring of a character on *Planet Of The Apes*. It is a sad day at ABC. We pride ourselves on our cultural diversity and have zero tolerance for bigotry. We can do better than this. You can do better than this.

All this being said, it has come to our attention, via a new intern at ABC Family, that Roseanne's statement may not have been bigoted at all. After all, the apes in the series are the superior, intelligent species who utterly dominate the mute, primitive humans. Hence, the comparison might easily be viewed as a compliment.

This looks bad for ABC. We should have probably kept *Roseanne* on the air, maintained our ratings, and used the above as a defense. But—too late. The damage has already been done.

Still, going forward, to prevent further misreadings and racism from being presumed where none exists, we are hereby outlining new protocols that clearly demarcate the boundaries of the offensive. This will help our creative and marketing teams immeasurably. The key element is to avoid racial conflicts at all costs, so that we can forevermore live in a kind of Shangri-La where we feel less white guilt about overseeing productions that hardly match the progressive tenor of the day. Anyway, here goes…

Phrases To Avoid

With all our programming (news broadcasts, sitcoms, talk shows), it is important that we pay close attention to the language used around people of color. The number one hot button issue to avoid is any intimation that African-Americans can be compared to apes. As a result of how sensitive this issue is we ask you all to be mindful about the topic in general, and, more specifically, remove the following phrases from your vernacular:

1) "Monkeying around." Example—A white character tells his black friend "stop monkeying around." No. We repeat no! It doesn't matter if this is a colloquialism. The word "monkey" should never be uttered in the vicinity of an African-American. The implications alone spell suicide for a broadcast. Alternatives include "fooling around," "messing around," and "joshing each other like silly pals." We also request you avoid "horsing around." Although people of color are not generally associated with horses there is a fear out there that we might be implying all black people are "black stallions," maybe even "dark and dangerous thoroughbreds." Furthermore, because we don't want to in any way associate people of color with animals, kindly refrain from referring to either Michael Jordan or LeBron James as the G.O.A.T.

2) "Let's go to the zoo." Example—A white character asks his black friend "let's go to the zoo." Again, this is way too incendiary a statement. Instead, have the white character ask to play soccer. (Note: Don't ask him to play basketball, for—duh—not all blacks are headed for the NBA).

3) "Darwin is inspirational." Don't say this. Just don't. It's the third rail of communication. In fact, when there is a person of color on your talk show or news program, don't ever bring up Darwin. Why? Because Darwin compared men to monkeys and there is a high degree of probability something inappropriate will be said about African-Americans once the subject is broached. As far as ABC is concerned there is no such thing as *On The Origin Of Species*. That's right. We're going with creationism. The world began 3000 years ago when Moses rode a triceratops up Mt. Sinai. Yes, here at ABC nearly everything in the Bible is utterly factual—including that weird Tower Of Babel story not even religious zealots take seriously.

Behaviors To Avoid

There are certain actions African-American cast members should never engage in while in an ABC Production. It is difficult to produce an exhaustive list, but, again, anything suggestive of a primate connection is heretofore banned. Troubling behaviors include a person of color pounding his chest, grunting, or, worst of all, consuming a banana (watermelon consumption is actually far less racist today).

Because the list of potentially toxic actions is so exhaustive we ask that all employees refer to their new 800 page guidebook, *Avoiding Racial Implications And Protecting The Disney Brand.*

The racially-charged situations your guidebook will help you navigate are not solely hypotheticals. Indeed, senior management is constantly getting vituperative complaints from fans of our shows who are seeking out the most subtle signs of racism in our programming and sharing them on Twitter, Reddit, and IG (to the dismay of our advertisers). At various times, then, we have had to consider shutting down hit shows (the *Roseanne* decision was not an isolated incident) even if the racism others perceived was entirely imaginary (we'd rather go bankrupt then be viewed as tone deaf).

Final Note: The cover for your guidebook happens to be a picture of Africa. We in no way are implying that our African-American employees need to go back to Africa. Instead, we wanted all employees to appreciate the wonders of Africa (including elephant poaching, blood diamonds, and violent military coups).

<u>Diverse Casting Vs. Averting Racist Implications</u>

While ABC is intent on putting a separation between African-Americans and primates, this impetus is counterbalanced by our emphasis on multicultural casting. What then is the Casting Director for say a jungle-based *TV Movie Of The Week* to do?

Picture it. The scene is Vietnam. Soldiers munch on strange, native fruits. Climb trees to obtain cover. Grunt and growl—often beating their chests like King Kong.

In such a situation we cannot simply eliminate all African-Americans from the production (for we believe in diverse casting). And yet, if we include soldiers of color acting like raging primates, we risk infuriating audiences.

Our senior management has concluded the only logical thing to do in this situation is eliminate all jungle scenes from said movie. It doesn't matter how integral they are to the plot. Audiences cannot withstand such highly toxic associations.

We have a war movie right now, based on Vietnam, that is going to take place entirely in a Whole Foods Market. Realistic? No! That said, Whole Foods, like the jungle, is rather green. In both there is fresh produce. What is more we really feel the production won't suffer in noticeable ways if, for example, the big death scene takes place between the aisles offering Homeopathic Medicine and Ayurvedic Shampoo.

Finally, as many of you know, our parent company, Disney, recently purchased the rights to *The Planet Of The Apes* franchise. Sadly, the backlash from Roseanne's tweet has been so severe that they have decided to pull all further *Planet Of The Apes* films. This is upsetting to us as it is to them. But, let's face it, probably also for the best.

The very idea of apes—dark apes—running wild—is simply too much of a hot button issue to ever associate ourselves with these films again. That said, we are being told that they are considering developing a new franchise, *Planet Of The Inferior Caucasians*, that should do well in the millennial market since it plays into the culturally-accepted notion of eternal fire and brimstone for evil whitey. Best of all the story is of such a saccharine nature that not even chronically-unemployed, virtue-signaling social justice warriors could possibly take offense.

Sincerely,

Howard Davine
Executive VP, *ABC Studios*

P.S. Whomever sent me that vile hate mail suggesting ABC stands for African Baboon Chimps will be fired immediately and prosecuted to the full extent of the law. In case it isn't readily apparent, ABC does not find crude ethnic jokes remotely amusing! So stop making them! We're owned by Disney for crying out loud! The company that made *Shrek 2*! And *Ratatouille*! Have some class you bunch of goddamn monkeys! Excuse me. I didn't mean that. You know what I meant! Behave yourselves—or you apes are gonna burn! Jesus! Did it again! Alright, I'll stop acting like a slave master! Damn! DAMN! DAMN! I GIVE UP!

Yelp Reviews Of The Crucifixion

CRUCIFIXION OF JESUS
***   1526 Reviews

***** 01/15/0000
Mordechi Y.

404 Friends
602 Reviews
0 Photos (Note: Camera Not Yet Invented)

I've always preferred a good crucifixion to *damnatio ad beastias*, or the feeding of a criminal to the lions. The problem with the latter is the crowd frequently grows delirious. "Kill him! Flog him! Rip him to shreds!" they roar, altogether making the spectacle rather corrupting, as Cicero once implied.

Thankfully, crucifixions are, comparatively speaking, highly-refined terminations of spirit. In my fifty-six years in Judea, I've had the good fortune to attend nearly two-hundred of them. Some involved the accused being impaled at the stake, others affixed to a tree, still others nailed to an upright pole and crossbeam.

Regardless of the methodology, I often find it rewarding—certainly moreso than playing dreidel in some murky cave. Then, too, I frequent these spectacles because the beer is cheap, the slaves friendly, and the squirming of the victim in a helpless state an undeniable spiritual emollient.

Still, no crucifixion has quite compared to that of Jesus H. Christ. I reveled in it all: the subtle lashings, that radiant crown of thorns, the methodical driving of nails into those tormented appendages. Moreover, I found it lamentable that he was hung between two thieves—for Jesus should in no way be compared to such lowly criminals (even if he occasionally stole plums from my cousin's stand in Galilee).

About my only regret was missing the resurrection. Unfortunately, my wife needed to get a blackened tooth extracted. Constantly she whined about her lip getting puffy. By the time we arrived at the burial grounds (where Jesus was placed in a new tomb by Joseph of Arimathea), his eminence had already soared into the clouds, leaving us at the mercy of a third-rate puppet show (that hardly provoked an Aristotelian catharsis).

In spite of this paltry setback, I feel it a five star crucifixion. Jesus certainly inspired us over the years with his capricious miracles (which surpass anything by Elijah, who, at best, brought fire down from the sky). His sermons further seemed on par with the best of our kabbalistic tradition—making us, at times, want to tour Judea with him and/or auction off his carpentry tools at a hefty premium.

At the same time, Pontius Pilate could not be blamed. It made sense that he responded so forcefully to an impudent rogue who fed thousands with five loaves of bread and two fish. For, as every denizen knows, when entertaining you need to at least roast a mountain goat!

We went on to drink wine by the barrel—there was hardly any water in Jerusalem that hadn't been magically transformed—feeling thankful that we'd gotten to witness a low-level prophet—on par with Micah The Morashite—get crucified in spectacular fashion. These were the kind of glories last experienced at the height of the Persian Empire.

Long Live Caesar Tiberius!

** 02/01/0000
Maximilus R.

176 Friends
19 Reviews
0 Photos (Note: Camera Still Not Invented)

The crucifixion of Jesus was a disgusting bore. I've witnessed debates on the floor of the Senate that were more lively. In the very least Pontius Pilate could have provided a lectus, so members of the disgruntled audience could take a nap!

Exacerbating matters was the three shekels I spent on front row seats. Talk about overpaying! Then there were those haughty beer wenches who languidly slugged over pitchers of noxious brew produced by doltish Babylonians. Worst of all, though, were the virulent knife fights at every last barter and trade station. Can't attendees at a crucifixion demonstrate a modicum of propriety?

My reading suggests the crucifixion of Spartacus and 6000 of his fellow insurgents along the Appian Way offered far better value (with crucifixions every ten minutes). Those were exalted days when men were less valued than rats! Watching Jesus squirm and moan, like a self-infatuated little alchemist, made me long for a return to the preeminent rule of Crassus!

The other conspicuous shortcoming was the dearth of blood. Honestly, this crucifixion was so devoid of the macabre fluid that I found myself longing for a routine beheading. This isn't to suggest there aren't other worthy execution methods—sawing, gibbeting, and cooking the prisoner on a gridiron all provide wholesome entertainment. Still, is anything comparable to a merciless beheading? Tongue protracted? Blood splattering crowds? Head passed from one set of hands to another like a boiling potato?

Exacerbating matters further, I travelled hundreds of miles by camel—a hoary, enfeebled camel mind you—to attend a crucifixion that started *eight hours after had been ordained in stone*. Get with the program you carve into rock, you haughty imbeciles!

Finally, Jesus stunk. Veritably, I say unto you, even five-hundred feet from his jaundiced body the stench wafted towards me with enough intensity to induce widespread panic!

This noxious body odor was further magnified by the frequent emptying of his bowels into the sand. If there was anything truly ungodly about this man it was the logs that went flying out his arse with eerie regularity. How malodorous! I give this crucifixion two stars—and that's being generous. What a fiasco!

* 02/18/0000
Yosef R.

42 Friends
7 Reviews
0 Photos (DM me via carrier pigeon for more info)

I travelled from Beersheba to see an inspiring spectacle. What I got was a wretched sob story. Poor Jesus up on the cross weeping all afternoon as if the lead in a Sophocles play. The Romans are right to expect more from an execution!

On multiple occasions, Jesus remarked: 'Forgive them father, for they know not what they do?' This is dumb. The Romans knew exactly what they were doing. Quelling a threat to the empire by a highly-delusional carpenter who should have stuck to plywood!

Next Jesus starts up with the 'why have you forsaken me?' How vexing! You're The Son Of God.

Act like it! After years of prancing around Judea forcing crowds to interpret parables that make absolutely no sense you're gonna start bawling like an infant? This is the year 0 A.D. Toughen up! Perform another miracle! I've met charioteers with ten times more resolve than you!

The only reason I even bothered to attend was Pontius Pilate put together an incredible marketing campaign. First he plastered catchy ads on fresh papyrus all over the town square. Next certain caves, where carnivals are held, had petroglyphs hyping up the day when the Roman Calendar would be reset (I was enthralled by the idea of time going from B.C. to A.D.). Finally, outside the Beersheba Market, voluptuous ladies in skimpy togas promised this would be the biggest execution since Aleppo The Butcher was fed to the dogs.

To be fair the crucifixion had its moments–such as when the crowd pelted Mary Magdalene with tomatoes (she was crying histrionically and deserved it). Others enjoyed when the town shoe cobbler suggested that the immaculate conception wasn't quite so immaculate (he joked about God defiling Mary atop Mt. Sinai).

Nevertheless, I would never have traversed so many lousy sand dunes had I known Jesus was gonna act like such a sniveling little brat. It was such a poor swan song that I requested a refund.

The jerk in the oversized tunic at the barter and trade hut told me 'complain and you're next on the cross.' Then my wife started weeping, claiming without a refund we'd starve on our trip back to Beersheba (little did the poor sap know I was flush with coins from selling Bedouins fake camel-riding licenses).

He seemed entranced by her melodramatic sentiment and was about to give us our shekels back, plus two all-you-can-eat-feasts on the couch of our choice, when a seamstress accused my wife of stealing her goat. Next thing you know Roman Soldiers whisked my wife away and beheaded her. I stood there, aghast, as the shoe cobbler compared the decapitated head of my wife to the corroded genitals of the town whore.

In sum—even given that I was never really all that fond of my wife to begin with—this was the worst execution I've ever attended. I give it 1 star and plead with you, dear reader, to find some other means of entertainment (even if it's just writing an epic poem in the style of *The Aeneid*). Faithfully, I say unto you, you're better off staying home and stabbing yourself in the chest with a poisonous spear!

Love Now Traded On The NYME

In a stunning move Fed Chairman Jerome Powell approved the addition of a new commodity, love, onto the New York Mercantile Exchange. Commodities like wheat, corn, soy beans, and pork bellies have long been pedaled on commodities exchanges. But due to its ethereal nature love was formerly unable to be traded by the bushel.

"We changed all that fast," said Jamie Dimon, C.E.O. of J.P. Morgan Chase. "Every American deserves the right to buy the love they could not obtain during childhood." Love—(traded under the symbol LUVV)—has instantaneously soared in value, particularly since therapists buy it in large quantities and sell it a premium to lonely clients.

Then there are romantics who quit writing poetry on dusty typewriters to become LUUV traders instead. "It's way easier than writing villanelles," said Pierre Leblanc, who claims to have seduced dozens of women by showing them his Charles Schwab brokerage statement.

But the most surprising fans are the thots who buy LUVV and then go on IG and post nude selfies next to a daily commodities chart. Some even leave comments under their picture such as, "OMG! my LUVV keeps growing!" Or "Damn! Every day is Valentine's!"

A final group intrigued by LUVV are icons from the countercultural revolution. "It's not free LUVV," the folk singer Joan Baez said, "but I don't mind paying a premium if it makes me feel like I'm shacking up with Dylan again." She then played the harmonica.

Analyst sentiment on LUVV is mixed. Jim Cramer, host of the CNBC show *Mad Money*, worries that investors will become addicted to the positive vibes LUVV engenders. "It's hard to dump LUVV," he said on the show *Fast Money*. "But sometimes you need to move in separate directions." He went on to warn that LUVV was an aphrodisiac, and suggested, when you're in bed together, that you "use a prophylactic," preferably one with a "spermicidal lubricant." He also recommends regular screenings for venereal diseases.

Critics, like hedge fund manager Roy Dalio, however, feel love is overvalued. "You can easily live without it," he claimed. "America is far more dependent on foreign sources of oil." He added that there is far greater domestic demand for low gas prices than for romantic getaways to the Poconos.

Perhaps the best aspect of LUVV trading on the market is that we have a better sense of what feelings are worth. A boyfriend who wants to break up with his girlfriend can now clearly assess the value of her broken heart (497.24$ plus commissions and brokerage fees). Then, too, polygamy has become more lucrative. Noted polygamist Warren Jeffs, infamous for marrying twenty wives, reportedly stated on a day when LUVV's value went up 85%, "today I became a very wealthy man."

Misanthropes, of course, have a very different perspective. When pressed for a comment, Terry Nichols, one of the architects of the Oklahoma City bombing, had this to say: "since when is love worth anything? Humanity is doomed."

MATT NAGIN

Matt Nagin is a writer, educator, actor, filmmaker, and standup comedian. Matt has taught college writing at seven universities in the NYC area, among them Fordham, Long Island University, and The Fashion Institute of Technology. In 2018, his poem, "If We Are Doomed," won The Spirit First Editor's Choice Award. Another poem, "Birds Singing In His Chest," was published in the anthology "New York's Best Emerging Poets 2019." He has two poetry books available on Amazon, "Butterflies Lost Within The Crooked Moonlight," and "Feast of Sapphires," both of which have obtained very strong critical and reader reviews. Kirkus Reviews, for example, referred to Matt's first book as "powerful verse from a writer of real talent."

Matt's first collection of humorous writings, "From the Fridge to the Crackerjack Box", was published in 2007, and since then he's had satirical work showcased in The Humor Times, The Satirist, Robot Butt, Points In Case, The Higgs-Weldon, The New York Post, and many others. He also wrote/directed a short film, "Inside Job," that won awards on the festival circuit, such as Best Short at The Mediterranean Film Festival Cannes and Best Supporting Actor at the Nice International Film Festival.

As an actor, Matt has appeared on a wide range of TV and film programs, most recently in a Co-Star role in a scene with Al Pacino, in a new Amazon series, "Hunters," produced by Jordan Peele. Matt has further performed standup in seven countries, on The Dr. Steve Show, The Wendy Williams Show, and at The Edinburgh Comedy Festival. A survivor of Crohn's disease, for thirty years, Matt was granted The Crohn's and Colitis Foundation's 2019 Mission Award.

CPSIA information can be obtained
at www.ICGtesting.com
Printed in the USA
JSHW021807011219
2718JS00004B/12

9 780648 480273